Momaya Annual Review
2007

A Momaya Press Publication

London, U.K. & Gaylordsville, Connecticut, U.S.A

First published in the United States of America, 2007 by Momaya Press. The moral right of Momaya Press has been asserted.

Printed and bound in the United States

ISBN 978-0-6151-7276-7

Table of Contents

Foreword   i

Manipura*   1

C is for Cuckoo*   11

From Tesco to Mother Earth   25

Dog Days*   31

Mr. Potato Head   39

The Aquarium*   45

Crazy*   51

Epiphany   59

Cry Baby *   65

Shredding the Label   73

Ash*   81

The Evangelist   89

Renovation (3rd Prize)   97

The Photographer (2nd Prize)   103

Quarry (1st Prize)   109

The Authors   117

The Photographer

The Judges

Momaya Press

Acknowledgements

* Honorable Mention

List of Illustrations

"Fireworks"

"Fruit Stand"   10

"Girl Sells Rocks"   24

"Water Dog at the Wharf"   30

"Shellfish"   38

"YMCA Pool"   44

"Swamp Barber Retires"   50

"Church Poster"   58

"Waterworks Building"   64

"Enfants Horibles"   72

"Shooting"   80

"Arraignment Close"   88

"Grace Charm School"   96

"Accident on Boston Street"   102

"Friendship in Salem"   108

Foreword

Welcome to the Momaya Annual Review 2007. We publish this anthology to showcase up and coming writers, many of whom have never been published before. We hope that this anthology will provide a platform to launch their literary careers, as well as provide an aspirational goal for potential writers. We publish solely short stories to promote this art form among readers and writers globally.

The writing contained in this publication was submitted to the Momaya Short Story Competition 2007. We received 204 entries to the competition (an increase of 8% over the 189 entries received in 2006). Our competition is open to English-language submissions from anywhere in the world. We were pleased to receive 2007 entries from sixteen diverse countries: Australia, Canada, Czech Republic, France, Germany, Greece, Guatemala, India, Ireland, Israel, Kenya, The Netherlands, South Africa, St. Vincent and the Grenadines, United Kingdom, and the United States of America. We encourage people to submit wherever in the world they may be, or whoever they may be. To insure the utmost impartiality, our judges do not see the name or contact information of the authors when they read the stories; they see just the title and text of the story when choosing the winners.

The 2007 theme of transformation proved to be fertile ground for our writers' imaginations. While entries for the short story competition were welcome on any fictional topic, the review gets its cohesion from stories, poems and artwork on this central theme. The short stories in this collection express the theme from the literal (á la Kafka) to the cerebral (the transition from childhood to adulthood). Overall, these stories highlight the power of transformation to change how we think of ourselves, others, and the world around us.

We would like to thank the judges who support Momaya Press and our mission to promote the short story. Three judges comprised the 2007 panel: Lucy Alexander, Alison Hennessey, and Claire Nozières. Lucy Alexander is a writer and researcher at The Times Magazine. Lucy was a PR account manager at Freud Communications before becoming a journalist. Alison Hennessey is an Assistant Editor at Random House. Claire Nozières works at Andrew Nurnberg Associates as a literary agent. Previously she was Foreign Rights Manager at Frances Lincoln, an independent publishing house specialized in high-quality illustrated books and children's books. Claire sells translations rights to France for a wide-ranging list of contemporary US and UK fiction.

This is the 4th edition of the Momaya Annual Review. You may see previous Short Story Competition winners and purchase previous year's editions of the Momaya Annual Review at our website. Our short story competition is open year-round and entries may be submitted via our website.

You will not see the work published here elsewhere. We encourage you to share this anthology with friends, families, and writers. We hope that our publication will inspire writers to write even more, and readers to put pen to paper. We welcome your entries in our future competitions.

Enjoy,

Maya Cointreau and Monisha Saldanha
Directors
Momaya Press
www.momayapress.com

Manipura

(Honorable Mention)

By Susan Davis

A few nights back, I dreamed of the Devil. The Devil is easy to recognise, handsome, with smouldering eyes and the crackle of hell-fire about him. His sartorial elegance is without equal. In my dream, he was wearing lizard-skin Oxfords, and a waistcoat made from the softest nubuck; a gold Rolex glittered among the black hairs of his wrist. Instead of a pitchfork, he twirled a silver-topped cane. I didn't see any horns. The Devil is far too subtle for that. If he beckons to you, you must *never, ever* follow. No matter how irresistible he seems.

I woke to find myself moist, fluttering inside. It's a frightening thing somehow, to wake alone in the dark, to find yourself aroused. There was such a strong smell of burning in the room that I had to go downstairs, wafting from room to room in my nightie, checking plugs and switches, last night's fire. Had I fixed the guard into place before coming to bed? Had I switched off the grill? It seemed like I had.

There was a lingering scent of charred toast, that was all. Otherwise everything was normal: the furniture static, well behaved in the moonlight.

I get like this when Gavin is away. I get fretful, always checking up on myself. As if I can't trust myself to do things right. Gavin is away from home a lot. He's an expert on natural resources, he tells people in the Third World how to make the most of what they've got. When he comes home he brings me gifts; silk scarves and wooden beads, crudely coloured woven mats, and once even some soapstone effigies. Unwrapping them, I feel like the spoiled greedy queen of a decaying empire. I know they are gifts to appease a lonely wife.

The Devil dream worries me a little. The next day I open all the windows. The November air carries with it that cindery smell of bonfires, of dead matches lingering. "It's just something lacking in your metabolism," Trudy's sharp-boned face looms over me, as I lie on her bed. She adjusts a Rose Quartz crystal on my sternum, close to my heart. "That's what your dream is telling you. That you lack fire-energy, that's "Manipura" in Hindu."

Gavin doesn't approve of Trudy. He says that New-Age therapists like Trudy make a fortune out of spoilt westerners like me. For all the good they do, I might as well consult one of the Tahitian witch doctors he came across on his last trip.

But I trust Trudy, talking so knowledgably about Chakras, and the ten-petalled lotus, which is my heart.

Trudy is painstaking in her explanations. "You know Lorna, it's the same as when pregnant women get a taste for coal. It's the body's way of telling them they've got an iron deficiency. That's what you've got, fire deficiency."

Trudy's prescription is simple. I should eat spicy foods, dress in vibrant colours, I should light candles in every room. I must put some sparkle into my life.

Should I blame Trudy then, for what happened next? Or should I blame the dream? Let me tell you first, so you will know whom to blame. Not me, Lorna, a name that goes with my limp fair hair, my forsaken look. I am forty-one. My children are grown up. You must understand that rarely am I bothered by pheromones or moon cycles.

I am, or I thought I was, content. In Gavin's absence, I do my embroidery, I grow lilies in pots, I retire early to my white bed with a glass of milk and a book. I'm not afraid to be alone in this cottage with its draughty chimneys, and tear-stricken windowpanes, its hungry great fireplaces which I sometimes complain of. (Until that is, Gavin reminds me of those women in the Sudan, who must walk six miles for their firewood, and then back for the water to boil on it).

"You don't know how lucky you are," he shakes his head, and I feel ashamed.

So I am fortunate. A fortunate woman. Nothing to do but wait for my husband to come home, bearing his gifts.

Still, it's hard work keeping warm. No matter how the fire blazes, I am cold inside. And all the time that scorched smell follows me; elusive, teasing. An acrid perfume. More fire, says Trudy. I follow her advice. I swap my limp salads for chillies that scald my tongue. I exchange my pale mohair sweaters for African prints, and the cool preludes of Bach for Brazilian jazz. I light candles until the house is lit up like a shrine. Then I sit by my fire in red flannel pyjamas, and roast my bare toes like chestnuts.

Shortly after my Devil dream, there's a phone call for me. A girl with the voice of a temptress out of a coffee advert, purrs at me, 'weell I take a call from Colombia, plizz?' Gavin comes on. "How's my girl?" he says vaguely.

"Fine. Keeping Warm. Gavin?"

"Yes?"

"There's nothing wrong with the circuiting is there, the electrics I mean?"

"Nothing at all, why?" , I feel his hackles rising, suspicious at once.

"Oh nothing," I sigh. "Just this smell of burning."

"Something in the air," Gavin says. "Bonfires probably. Bloody neighbours are always lighting bonfires." He goes on about pollution, and global warming, and bids me good night.

Things go wrong when Gavin is away from home. It's as if the house knows, and sets traps for me, out of spite. Once, the bedroom ceiling came down, another time, the pipes froze. I tread warily about my house, like a thief, afraid to touch, to spark things off.

One night, just as I'm about to set a match to the fire, there is the soft thud of falling soot, a fierce scrabbling in the chimney. The bird must be big, a magpie perhaps, a jackdaw? I dread its appearance in the hearth, jack crow beating its great sooty wings, clawing the furniture, its coal black eyes glittering at me.

I fish behind the clock, and here are the cards left by Gavin in case of emergencies: emergency plumbers, carpenters, electricians, and the one I'm looking for......

FIRE WORKS

Nick Olds, Chimney Sweep

Chimneys cleaned, re-lined, bird cowls fitted

Traditional brush method. Personal service.

Nick Olds arrives within the hour. He looks more like a biker than a sweep, crackling in black leather, smelling of soot. As he stoops to screw his rods, a lava-flow of hair, black dreadlocks, tumbles, tangles; it's as if something wild, not house-trained, untrustworthy. The crow itself drags its feathers on the hearthrug; the hearthrug, which Gavin brought back from his last trip, hand-woven by Ethiopian tribes-women.

"Bird is it?" His voice is as hoarse as the parched raven. "Don't worry darling. We'll soon shift him."

Darling? I decide not to object. He is that kind of man, the kind who calls all women 'darling'; old, young, beautiful, ugly.

The stage is set: dustsheets in place, the flat spiral brush like a ridiculous wig. With a thrust or two the bird is dislodged. It brings down an avalanche of soot. I wonder aloud what kind of bird it was.

"Not a crow I hope, for your sakes darling," says Nick. His eyes are smoky behind the lava-locks. "You know what a crow in the chimney means?"

"No. No, I don't."

"Death," he says.

Afterwards, I think I must have summoned the crow and with it the chimney sweep, as if by incantation. The candlelight, the crimson lamps, the hot Latin rhythms, until the whole house is bubbling like a cauldron. An accidental spell. Abominable words tripped from the tongue, to summon Demons.

The trouble is, I can't stop thinking about Nick the Sweep, his elegant thrusts and brush-twirlings. It's as if I've known him forever, from another life. As if he's an old flame. Alone, in front of my fire, I want to strip to my skin and tango naked. In my imagination I am shameless. I crawl on all fours. I present myself to him. I am hot, hot, hot. A bitch on heat.

I go to see Trudy. "Whatever you did with my chakras," I plead with her, "can you turn it down a notch or two? Can you turn down the heat?"

Trudy shakes her head. "Can't be done. I won't meddle with the mysteries of Manipura."

I am amazed. Angry. Has Trudy, my guru, my precious ally, my confessor, turned against me? She can't treat me today anyway, she says. She is washing her crystals to cleanse them of unwelcome vibrations. Chunks of Rose Quartz, of purple Amethyst, poke like lost islands from the soapy suds.

"It's not like me though," I point out, temper rising. I want to smash her crystals, hurl them into space. "It's like an itch. A pain. And the smell of burning everywhere I go, as if it's my own flesh singeing."

At this, Trudy lifts something from her crystal-bath, a knobble of stone, greenish-black. "Look. D'you know what this is?"

I shake my head, dismayed.

Obsidian is volcanic rock, cooled molten lava, Trudy tells me. "Volcanoes can lie dormant for a thousand years. It's like they're playing dead. Yet, deep down below the surface, who knows what's going on? Suddenly, when you least expect it, whoosh!"

"But…I don't want to go woosh! I was happy enough before. All right, not happy. Who's happy? I was comfortable. Content."

"Content!" Trudy scoffs. As her fingers close over the Obsidian, I have a feeling that it's my own heart she cradles, that Trudy is playing games with my heart.

A few nights later, and he's back again. At first I think it's insects, but the night air is thick with smuts and cinders whirling, as if from a thousand bonfires. As I open the door I look in vain for the moon, but she's gone, smoked-out.

An after-service check, Nick Olds says, and how does my chimney seem? "Not smoking is it? No more crows, jackdaws? No storks?"

"Not that I know of." I try to sound cool. "You haven't brought your brushes."

"I brought this instead." He holds up a bottle of Tequila. "Warm your cockles. Cosy place you've got here darling. Snug." He is already draped in the Parker-Knoll, Gavin's chair by the fire. He takes a swig from the bottle, passes it to me. I drink and it's like swallowing fire. I can taste the brand of his lips on the bottle's neck.

"Where's the old man then, tonight?" He lights a cheroot, blows smoke-rings like a conjuror's trick.

"He's doing good works in other lands." I giggle. "He's a bit of a saint actually."

We laugh at this. This is how wicked I am this night. The truth is I am thinking of my saintly Gavin, presenting his trophies, lordly, munificent. That look in his eye, as if he would wish me otherwise; strong, enduring, a native-woman, bundles of firewood beneath each arm, a pitcher of water on my head.

"How d'you know?" Nick says. When he smiles he is handsome as the devil. "What he gets up to over there. So many miles away. No man is a saint."

When she touches me, Trudy flinches. "Ouch! You're burning-up. I can't treat you with fever," she helps me up from the bed, "sorry Lorna, can't be helped. It confuses the energies."

Trudy's crystals have an extra sparkle to them now that she's washed them. They glow rosy in the lamplight. Incense burns in little jars.

"But you must, you must do something. I'll pay you. I'll pay double." I tell her about Nick Olds, how he comes almost every night, his bottle of tequila, his cheroots, his smoky eyes.

Trudy just sighs and tells me about a woman she once treated for depression. "Her husband was away a lot too, something in oil, the Arab Emirates. She was so cold all the time, yet, she couldn't rid the house of this smell, as if the air itself was scorching.

"Then one day a friend called round and found her, or rather part of her. A lower limb, ankle singed at the edges, shoe intact, lying there on the hearthrug. The rest, ashes."

"What are you telling me? What?" I whisper, almost scalding myself with my own breath.

Trudy leans close. She hisses as if the walls have ears. "You've never heard of... *spontaneous combustion*? She burned out, you see, from the inside. Do you get what I'm saying Lorna? From the inside."

There is a call from Colombia when I get home.

"I don't know how to tell you this," Gavin says. But he tells me anyway, about his interpreter on the project, a woman called Elena who lives in a tin shack with no running water. Elena supports her entire family on her pitiful earnings.

"You can't believe how these people live." Gavin's voice has natural gravitas. He has the worthy, faintly accusing tone of a news commentator, reporting on some distant atrocity. The thing is, Gavin says, pausing to clear his throat, he and Elena have become very close, and well, Elena needs him more than I do. I have everything I want surely? And not to worry, he will see to it that I'm "comfortable".

"Of course the house will have to be sold," Gavin says, "actually why don't you give the agent a call? We'll need a valuation. The sooner we get the house on the market the better. No sense in letting things drag on."

"Is she beautiful?" I ask him.

"Sorry?"

"Is she beautiful? I mean as well as being a saint and everything."

Gavin says tetchily that the Columbians are certainly a fine-looking people, but that looks have nothing to do with it, and he's sorry I should have to stoop to making such snide comments, but he supposes that's only to be expected.

He coughs again. "Look, Lorna, don't make it difficult for me, please. These things happen. I'll be over as planned, end of the month. I'll need to pick up some of my belongings of course. Don't worry, I'm not bothered about the furniture, you can keep that...."

I stand there listening. I don't scream or cry or spontaneously combust, none of those things. How does one compete with a saint after all?

Last night I dreamt of the Devil. He led me by the hand, down, down as if in an elevator, to the very bowels of the earth. There was so much activity down there, the glowing ruby caverns, the endless stoking of fires. And every so often explosions that threatened to tear the earth apart, great convulsions of rock and lava, and gasses, a boiling over-flow of living flame.

I padded downstairs, and set a match to the living room fire. There weren't many logs in the basket but who needs logs? Amazing how well they burned, the rain forest fruit bowls, the Mexican scarves, the African beads sizzling like tiny skulls. The seedpod maracas spat all over the room like a child's popgun. I laughed as I hurled them on, laughing and choking in the black smoke.

The clothes came next. Gavin's of course. The Indian cotton shirts hissed like snakes. I have to say the Panama hat was a disappointment, the way it slowly smouldered, as if Gavin's head was still in it, frowning at me. I wasn't having that. I had to help it along a bit with his papers, those travel journals he always kept so meticulously, his notes, his graphs and maps, the entire contents of his office really.

Next came the furniture, though that wasn't my doing. By now the fire would have its own way. It was licking the sofa cushions as I stumbled from the house.

"All right darling?" Nick Olds was out there, waiting for me. His kisses branded me like cigarette burns, his fingers walking smut marks on my skin.

I ran my fingers through the woolly spools of his hair. I'm no longer afraid to feel the horns there, like antlers budding.

C is for Cuckoo

(Honorable Mention)

By Cally Taylor

I snatch the shopping list from David and crumple it up. We have been arguing about what fruit to buy for the last two minutes and my wig is starting to itch. I roll the list into a ball and drop it onto the floor. David holds up his hands in surrender.

"I was only saying, Susan, that everything we need for the barbeque is on the list. Last year half the strawberries rotted away."

I pick up a melon and put it in the shopping trolley. I add another. David looks at them and then back at me. I raise my eyebrows at him.

"What?"

"Do we really need two, Susan?"

"Melon is good for you."

The expression on David's face changes.

"Well in that case... if the herbalist said that melon..."

"Cures cancer?"

"Don't be facetious, that's not what I meant."

"Maybe I should get three."

David humphs and picks up the crumpled shopping list. I push the trolley towards the meat aisle. We're in the car, driving home with a boot full of food, discussing who's coming to the barbecue. David is reeling off the list.

"Dave, Beth, Anna and Jessica have all confirmed."

"Who?"

"My Uni lot."

David's eyes are fixed on the road; he barely blinks. His back is straight and his hands are ten-to-two on the steering wheel. Even after all these years he still drives with perfect posture and positioning. He likes everything just so, perfect, like the bloody barbecue.

"Not the others. Who's Jessica?"

"I must have mentioned her. She used to hang round with me Dave, Beth.... "

"She was one of your Uni friends?"

"Kind of."

"What do you mean kind of?"

"Well. She joined the Drama society in my last term."

"Then why invite her to the barbecue, David?"

"She moved back from Australia recently and thought she'd look a few of us up on that school reunion site. We all got together in a chat room, talked, swapped Drama memories, you know? I thought she'd like to see everyone again so I invited her along today."

I look out of the window, watch the familiar streets stream by. I look back at David.

"Have you ever fucked her?"

When we get home I check on the kids; Amy is asleep in her cot and Jake is in front of the television, as usual. He started school last autumn but he still looks so small; just inches from the screen, the headphones jammed over his little head. I crouch near him. His eyes grow wide as a lion pounces on a prowling hyena and kills it with a swift bite to the neck. I identify with the lion. The programme ends and Jake jumps when he notices me. He pulls the headphones from his head and throws his arms round my neck.

"Hi Mummy."

"Hi yourself, David Attenborough."

"David who? Where's Granny?"

"She went home. She would have said goodbye but she didn't want to interrupt your programme."

"You're not going anywhere are you, Mummy? "

"No, button. We've done the shopping and Daddy's going to light the barbecue soon."

"That's not what I meant."

"What did you mean, Jake?"

Jake frowns and rubs his soft hands over my head before he presses his face into my neck.

"Nothing."

I pull him to me and bury my face in his hair. Jake lets me hang onto him for a few minutes and then jams the headphones back on. When I look up David is standing at the door.

"Susan. Can I have a word?"

We wander into the garden and admire the tea lights David has placed in small ceramic pots around the borders. It's chilly and I rub at my arms. David takes off his cardigan and wraps it around my shoulders.

"How many time did you shag her, David?"

"Why does it matter? It's past history."

"Is four years ago past history? Perhaps we could invite her too. They can have a fight about who gets to warm my side of the bed when I'm six feet under."

"That's not fair."

"Fair? I'm not the one who who's invited an old fuck buddy to our family barbecue."

David sighs.

"I shouldn't have invited Jessica," he says. "I didn't think."

"No, you didn't. That's your problem."

I can tell David's biting his tongue. That annoys me. I watch as he stands up, walks to the other side of the garden and then returns.

"Look," he says. "I don't want another argument about this. I tried to ring her earlier to put her off."

"But?"

"No answer and there wasn't an answerphone either so I couldn't leave a message."

"So she's still coming?"

"As far as I know, sorry."

"Is that all you can bloody say? Sometimes sorry isn't good enough, David. Sorry doesn't make everything right."

"I know. I'm...."

I'm putting the garlic bread in the oven when the doorbell goes. The combination of kitchen heat and the wig are making my head sweat. I want to pull it off, to wear my scarf or nothing at all but I can't because some bloody stranger has attached her finger to my doorbell.

"Hello," she says, "you must be Susan. Sorry I'm so early."

Jessica is tall, about 5'8", blonde with an agreeable face. She's also about six months pregnant.

"You must be Jessica."

I offer her a glass of orange juice and we drift into the garden and pause on the decking. We both watch David faff around with the barbeque until he looks up.

"Jessie! Hello!"

My husband speeds across the garden and wraps Jessica in an awkward hug. When he catches my eye he lets her go.

"Sit down, sit down," he says. "You've already got a drink, I see."

Jessica smiles and lowers herself into the seat that David has dragged across the decking. There are now deep welts in the wood. We only had it laid four months ago.

"You'll sit down too won't you Susan?" Jessica calls. "You probably need a rest."

I put a hand to my wig and smooth a stray hair from my eyes.

"A rest?"

Jessica's smile falters.

"From all the cooking. I didn't mean your...."

She looks at my hair and then her eyes flick away. David must have told her. I pull up a chair and force a smile.

"It's fine. I could do with a five-minute sit-down before everyone else arrives."

Jessica has small eyes, sly eyes - little pin pricks beneath hooded lids, circled with too much eyeliner. I watch as she looks at the garden and then her eyes flicker over the house. A small smile crosses her lips.

"You have a lovely home, Susan."

"Thank you."

Jessica nods. Now she's watching David as he prods the barbeque.

"David looks so well," she says. "Family life must agree with him."

I laugh. David is the sickliest man on the face of the planet. If he hasn't got a cold, he's got hayfever. If it isn't hayfever it's the flu or athlete's foot or conjunctivitis.

"Yes."

"And you have two children?"

"Jake's six and Amy is five months."

"How lovely."

I look pointedly at her bump.

"Do you have any other children?"

"No. Just this one."

I need her to look at me. I need her to look at me and stop staring at my husband.

"David tells me you've recently moved back to the UK. I imagine you and your husband wanted to be closer to your family for the birth?"

Jessica shifts in her seat. Her right hand reaches for the fourth finger of her left hand. Her fingers stroke bare skin.

"Not really. I've come back to be closer to my friends, and family, but Brian's staying in Australia. We separated a few months ago, but everyone has been so supportive, particularly David. Oh! That must be little Jakey."

I follow Jessica's eye line towards the kitchen door. "Little Jakey' is sucking his thumb, looking anxiously around the garden.

"Jake," I shout. "Come here and say hello to Daddy's friend."

Jake ambles over, one hand to his mouth, the other in his hair.

"Jake, this is Jessica."

Jessica opens her arms, offering a hug, but Jake turns away and buries his head in my armpit. Jessica reaches for my hand and squeezes it.

"It must be very hard, for you all," she says. "Is there's anything I can do?"

Her eyes are brimming with tears. I am horrified.

"Could you give me a minute please, Jessica? I think Jake is overtired."

I pick Jake up and lug him towards the kitchen.

"David, could I have a quick word?"

When I've settled Jake back in front of the television I go back into the kitchen. David has a finger in his mouth and he's frowning at the bowl of chicken marinade on the counter.

"What's going on, David?"

"Did you put extra salt in the marinade? It doesn't taste right."

I walk over to the counter, pick up the bowl of marinade and throw it at the sink. David grabs a tea towel and starts to mop at the dark stains on the stainless steel.

"David, did you hear me?"

"Huh?"

David crouches and rubs at the kitchen floor. I snatch the tea towel from his fingers.

"Would you stop?"

"Susan. What the hell? Keep your voice down. We've got guests."

"Guest."

I slam the kitchen door shut and turn to face my husband.

"What is that woman really doing in our garden? In our home?"

"I told you. She's come for the barbecue."

"And what else?"

"Nothing. Susan you're not making sense. Do you need a lie down? Maybe the barbecue was a mistake."

I pick up a glass from the kitchen table and throw it at him. David deflects it with his hand and it smashes on the floor. David walks towards me, his arms outstretched.

"Don't touch me, David."

He stops. I can't bear the pained expression in his eyes but I can't stop myself.

"That woman knows everything about us, everything about me and she has not come here for a barbecue."

"Then what has she come here for Susan?"

"For you. For my family. For my home."

"Oh for God's sake. Are you mad?"

"No, David. No, David I'm not mad. You tried that line on me before, remember? And I wasn't mad. I was right."

David winces.

"Susan. That was years ago. Please don't. Not now."

"You may not be having an affair with Jessica now, but you will. At least have the decency to wait until I'm dead."

David crumples. He loses a good two inches in height before my eyes.

"Susan. Don't. God."

Something inside me rages and screams.

"Look at her David. She's six months pregnant. She leaves her husband and comes back to Britain. Who does she look up? An old fuckbuddy from Uni, someone she's probably always held a torch for and guess what, his wife is only dying of cancer. It couldn't be more perfect, could it? Little ready-made home, ready-made brother and sister, ready-made husband. She just has to hang on until I die and then it's all hers."

David says nothing. He just stands two feet away from me and stares at my face. I can't bear to look him in the eye. I feel like I'm being ripped apart.

"What was it Robert Louis Stephenson said, David? 'The cruelest lies are often told in silence'. Maybe Jessica will have more to say for herself?"

I open the door to the garden.

"You," I say, pointing at Jessica.

She points to her chest even though there is no one else around.

"Me?"

"Yes you, you fucking cuckoo."

She looks past me and mouths, "David?"

I push my husband back into the kitchen and stride towards her. I have to fight the urge to grab her by both shoulders and push her and the garden chair she's wedged into, into the borders.

"Have you come here to steal my husband?"

"Susan, that's ridiculous. I'm pregnant for God's sake."

"Oh yes, so you are. We can hardly fail to miss it can we? Looking for a new nest are you? One that's already feathered? One where the mother bird is more likely to cark it than put up a fight?"

Jessica reaches a hand towards me but I ignore it.

"No. Susan. You've got it all wrong. I would never do that. Look, I'm sorry for your troubles but..."

Jessica puts her hands on the armrests and tries to push herself up. I push her back down.

"Oh no you don't."

Jessica starts to shout loudly, repeating my husband's name over and over again. There are footsteps and a hand on my back guides me onto the grass. It presses my shoulder until I sit down.

"I think perhaps Jessica should go now," David says.

Jessica sighs as she gets up from the chair and I look down, stare at the grass. When I raise my head again David is by my side.

"What the hell was that all about, Susan?"

David's voice goes right through me. There is a noise, a loud screaming voice. It sounds like mine but it's uncontrollable.

"She was going to take everything away from me and she was going to do it right in front of my face."

"No, Susan, she wasn't. She was here for some emotional support and you just screamed in her face."

I dig my nails into his shoulders.

"You invited her. You didn't think."

"No, no I didn't. For the split second it took to invite Jessica to the barbecue I didn't think. I thought everything was normal. There was no affair, there was no cancer, there was just you and me, having a barbecue, inviting our friends."

There are tears in David's eyes but I can't stop shaking him. David grips my hands. Sweat beads in his hairline.

"Susan," he says softly. "This isn't really about Jessica is it?"

Something inside me crumples and folds. I'm so tired of being sarcastic, defensive and 'fine'. I'm tired of pretending I'm not scared. David lets go of my hands and grabs hold of me. He holds me so tightly I can barely breathe.

"David," I whisper, "what if I'm the one that's stolen away?"

A small hand taps mine. It's Jake, a look of concern on his face.

"Mummy," he says. "What noise do lions make?"

"Roar."

"No, that's not right. It's too quiet. Do it properly."

I take a deep breath and roar at the top of my lungs. Jake smiles.

"Now we all do it. Daddy, you too."

David and I exchange a look. A bellowing roar fills the garden. Birds fly from the trees and fill the sky.

"That's better," says Jake. "Much better. Very good."

From Tesco to Mother Earth

By Judy Walker

I'm standing in the dark in the middle of a field on a hot July day, knowing that any minute now I'm going to have to say something really profound about why I'm here and what I hope to achieve.

At times likes this I tend to get the giggles but I don't think that would go down too well here. Someone – I think it was Andrea – has just said she wants to free herself of the negative energy that builds up every time her baby son cries at night and, before that, Pam – I'm pretty sure it was her – said she sought empowerment at work.

How middle class can you get? Ten women paying good money to sweat like gym whores in a makeshift tent of sticks while some South American guru tells them everything will be fine and dandy if they do a bit of humming.

I close my eyes (be serious! I admonish myself) then open them again. With a theatrical flourish Xaidiki sprinkles sage leaves and water onto the hot stones that are piled in the middle of the "sweat lodge'. The stones hiss and steam.

I can feel beads of perspiration running down me like flies spiders at sports day. I wonder if Alison would have even mentioned this to me if I didn't happen to live in a house with a field for a back garden.

"He's just the most marvelous person." She started telling me about Xaidiki while we picked over mangoes in the organic section at Tesco.

"He builds a sort of wigwam out of branches and ferns and…well, stuff like that and, because it's completely dark, it's all totally anonymous, so it frees you up to say what you really feel. It's sort of womblike. The energy is amazing."

"Oh yes?" I squeezed a likely looking candidate and was about to drop it into my basket when I noticed that Alison was sniffing her mango. I did the same.

"The thing is, you need a big enough space to build the sweat lodge."

"Sweat lodge?"

"Yes," her mango was obviously up to snuff because she peeled off a bag and dropped the fruit inside. "He heats up stones on a fire outside, then takes them in to the sweat lodge and pours water over them so it gets really hot – like a sauna - and because it's dark the atmosphere is – you know," she looked around then whispered in the direction of my ear, "intense."

"Right." I rolled my mango around between my palms. It felt clammy and slightly sticky. "So…the idea is…?" I looked her straight in the eye.

She shrugged her shoulders. "Oh, you know, self fulfillment, cleansing – it's very powerful."

I squeezed my mango then placed it slowly, bagless, into my trolley. *Today I will be confident, I will be successful, I will be my own person.* I repeated my mantra over and over as usual.

As I approached the checkout, I spotted Alison chatting to her cashier like they were best mates. I locked eyes with my girl, and smiled. She was chubby with bitten nails and wore a silver necklace with the letter "P" dangling from it.

"Clubcard?" she hissed, palm out. I opened my mouth, shut it and scrabbled in my purse. She extracted the card from my hand as if removing something not quite nice from the sole of her shoe, swiped it and returned it to me in one fluid, practiced movement. When she came to my mango she pinched it between her sausage fingers.

"What's this, a kiwi is it?" she growled.

"Er, no, a mango," I apologized.

"Organic?"

I confessed that it was.

She sighed and snatched at a laminated card, ran the stub of her finger down the colored pictures, then stabbed the appropriate keys on her machine and punched a sticker into the skin of my mango.

As I was loading my groceries into the boot of my car, Alison sprinted over.

"So…will you think about it – the sweat lodge?" she beamed, placing a hand on my forearm and lowering her voice: "I really think you'd get a lot out of it Kate."

"Yes, ok – let's go for it." Did I say that? I'm such a pushover I thought as I drove towards the exit, returning Alison's cheery wave. Maybe the sweat lodge is just what I need. Womblike she said, so perhaps if I can get back to the womb I can start my life all over again and get everything right this time. I like the sound of that.

Today I will be confident, I will be….

My skin is actually feeling very good I realize – soft and cleansed, like a well laundered blouse. I touch my cheeks and arms, enjoying their silky texture. Next time I go to the sauna I might try taking a few sage leaves along with me. I don't have sage in my herb garden but I've got a bay tree – maybe those would do.

I remember Alison enthusing at length about the earth thing. "The whole experience is very spiritual Kate but it's also very….organic. It makes you realise what the earth gives you and what you get out of it. It's immensely powerful." She sipped her coffee. "He's got a website and a CD too."

I asked her what she thought she'd got out of it – the experience, not the earth or the website. She stood up – we were sitting at my kitchen table at the time – and threw her head back, not unlike Xaidiki just did, and said: "I was transformed, totally and utterly transformed."

There's not a lot you can say to that, so I offered her another fig roll and took two myself. I get a bit embarrassed when people go spiritual on me, which is why I decided I needed something like this Sweat Lodge to take me beyond that and into a different place.

Xaidiki is a small, stocky South American. He reminds me of a troll, not because he's ugly, more to do with his pot belly and slightly bandy legs. The only item of clothing he wears is a pair of faded red shorts, rather short shorts in the style of a 70s footballer. He begins to semaphore his arms over the hot stones and chants a blessing. Then he throws his head back and reaches upwards with his arms, as if he's climbing a rope. This must be the calling up of the spirits that Alison told me about when she talked me through the whole "experience'.

I think it's about now that I should be starting to feel some sort of connection with mother earth but all I can feel is a burning in my throat from the heat. I cough as quietly as I can manage but unfortunately Xaidiki takes it as a hint that I want to speak and interrupts his chanting abruptly.

I try to summon up something – anything – to say. I am saved by another voice, which I recognize as Alison's – saying she is experiencing a real connection between herself and nature. I clench my fists and squeeze my eyes shut again. I think I'm just about the only one who hasn't spoken yet. Oh God, or mother earth, or someone, help me.

Xaidiki begins again in a sing-songy chanting tone. The sweat lodge is the womb of Mother Earth apparently, a place where we can re-connect ourselves to our minds, bodies and spirits. It is a place for self-healing from the stress and emotions of everyday living. What a load of bollocks. I don't think this is for me after all. I wonder if I can sneak out without anyone noticing – or even if they do I don't think I even care.

I take a deep breath in and the hot aroma of the sage fills my lungs. I can feel it inside my body scurrying into joints, down veins and through fibrous ligaments and into my ears, where it screams like a kettle till I have to put my hands over my ears to try to stop the noise. I close my eyes and as I do a whole video of images plays in my head – my mother coming towards me, a door slamming, a hospital ward with serious looking doctors, a teenager in a car, a small child on her own at the beach, my mother again but young this time. I feel dizzy, can't get my breath and I sit down heavily onto the ground. The grass feels hot to my touch and I spread out my palms onto it, sink my head onto the earth, slip back into the womb.

I'm aware of Xaidiki still talking about how the earth will speak to us and our hearts will cry out, helping us to connect, listen, heal. Oh my God, the earth has spoken to me and I've listened. I've had a spiritual awakening, haven't I? I've got to get out of here. As I stand up I hear a voice say:

"Today I will begin again." It's my voice and I have a horrible feeling I'm going to buy Xaidiki's CD. I wonder if Tesco stocks it.

Dog Days

(Honorable Mention)

By Joanne Riccioni

Summers in Italy were never as foreign as her grandfather. The summer Carolina turned five, Nonno took her cheek between his woody thumb and forefinger, like a fruit from his vines, and squeezed out tears. He laughed then and she had to kiss the shattered glass of his cheeks, hold her breath against his bonfire and vinegar smell, try to miss the yellow spit that curdled at the corners of his mouth.

The summer she was seven, they played a game. Nonno wrapped fish wire round her wobbly front tooth and tied it to the allotment gate. She was waiting for the fun part when she heard the gate slam and tasted the blood in her mouth like an old coin. All night she waited for the prize, twisting her tongue through the throbbing gap where her tooth had been. But they didn't have the tooth fairy in Italy.

The summer Carolina was eleven, Nonno killed her dog.

She and Uncle Vinny had found the puppy the summer before. Picnicking under the chestnut tree at Monte Lupo, Uncle Vinny had been teasing her that mortadella was donkey meat. She was laughing and poking at her panino when three tears skimmed her cheek. High in the branches above her head, a Hessian sack dripped and trembled, creaking softly. Uncle Vinny slashed it with his paring knife and out tumbled Pipo, mewling, all head-over-paws. On the pitted chalk road down the mountain, his tiny heart fluttered in her hand. She puzzled over the wet sack. You didn't come across things like that on picnics in East Anglia . She asked Uncle Vinny. He laughed through his nose and took his massive hand from the wheel to cup Pipo's head.

"Animals have a use here, Caroli'. There aren't many pets." Pipo whimpered and twitched in his sleep, his ears petals on her fingers.

"Didn't you have a dog when you were a boy here, Uncle Vinny?" she asked.

"Oh, I had a dog alright. Best dog you could ever have, that Rondinella." His shiny head slipped back on his shoulders and his eyes looked somewhere far beyond the pocked road ahead. "She looked a bit like a Collie, but we didn't really know about breeds back then. I found her as a puppy, all dirty and hungry, wandering the Vigna Nuova – hardly left my side until the day she died." He shook his shiny head and she heard him humming the faint tune of remembering.

"Me and your dad, we slept up at Colle Lungo during the War, in a big barn on the hill where we kept all the pigs. 'Course, Nonno had been caught in Tobruk and had already been shipped to Bedford by then. Nonna was busy trying to feed us all and thought it was safer for us kids up in the mountains away from the Germans when things got nasty. We slept in the straw and Rondinella was our blanket, even dragged in a rabbit sometimes for our dinner. One day – I was about your age – some Nazi soldiers took away our donkey. Nonna wailed and pulled her hair because that donkey was the only way we could get maize across the hills to Cori to trade. We had to eat the same old polenta day after day – no cheese, no salt, no oil. Can't stomach polenta even now." He stuck out his tongue, squinted an eye, rippled his expansive stomach for her amusement.

"That night Rondinella went missing. I made myself hoarse calling, but she didn't come. A few weeks later, me and your dad were feeding the pigs when we heard this barking. There was our donkey trotting up the dirt track and yapping at her hooves was Rondinella. She'd found the donkey and led it home, you see? Just like *Lassie*, eh?"

In her child's imagination, Pipo followed in the footsteps of the famous partisan dog, Rondinella. Carolina had visions of him protecting her from snakes in the grasses that hissed all the way to the fig tree at the Vigna Alba; or leading her safely through the ghosts that fluttered in the branches of the chestnuts when she swam too late in the lake at Carpineto. But also in her youthful mind, Italian summers drifted like the endless Viale Roma shimmering vaguely down between the scribbled hills and she gave no thought to what would become of Pipo when she had to take that road home again.

She fed the puppy on milky bread and smuggled him into her bed at night. He grew wolfish and ate everything in three chokes. He could run like a colt and hang frozen ten feet in the air to catch a stick. Nonna howled at him day and night for trampling through the tomato plants and Carolina tried not to hear the dull thud of Nonno's boot, Pipo's blank whimpers whenever her back was turned. Uncle Vinny built him a kennel and she painted it with his name in blood red letters. But the following summer the kennel had been upturned and in it a tangle of petunias, impatiens and zucchini were all fighting for space – Nonno's proud English annuals at war with the need to feed.

Nonno pinched her cheek and looked away when he saw her that first day of her eleventh Italian summer. Uncle Vinny drove her to the Vigna Alba where Pipo had been chained because of his incessant bark. Through the chalk dust thrown up by the car, she saw a corrugated lean-to and beneath it a rangy cur, its scabbed fur draped like the pelt of some other animal over its hip bones and ribs, eyes encrusted with flies. "Pip?" she snatched through her breath, willing it to be some other animal. Pipo's eyes tracked her as he heaved his feeble carcass to a sway, his desiccated coat rippling and shuddering in a tenuous life of its own. Uncle Vinny didn't see her crying. He had turned away, busy filling a bucket with ripe figs from the buzzing tree.

That night they hosed Pipo down and watched him inhale three bowls of rancid meatballs. Then they fixed up a new kennel in the shade of the *forno* and she used her Abba beach towel to make him a bed. At dinner, she asked Uncle Vinny what had happened to Rondinella. Nonno was under the pergola eating squares of watermelon from the tip of his paring knife. He sucked the juice through prehistoric teeth and clamped the knife between lifeless, petrified fingers. She thought of the volcanic remains of ancient Romans Uncle Vinny had taken her to see at Pompeii.

"*Si, si*, Vincenz', tell Carolina what happened to that dog." He hummed a phlegmy laugh.

"Papa …" Uncle Vinny breathed softly and leaned back in his chair, looking across the valley to the village rooftops cobbled between the dusky hills.

"I had a dog once too, you know, Caroli'?" Nonno's voice rolled in his chest, the Italian words rumbling up as if over shingle. His small, black eyes darted with purpose. "In the prisoner of war camp in Suez the English officers adopted a little dog. They called it Abdul after their mess cook. Fed it kitchen scraps we would have sold our mothers for. Two months they kept us there, frying by day, freezing by night, only let out of the compound to bury our dead." He paused to loosen his chest and machine gun watermelon seeds into the dirt. "In between times, we'd listen to that dog yapping at the officers' table. One night, Aldo Reggiero, a joker from Calabria, tempted it to the compound fence with a ball of rags. When the mutt got near enough I shoved my hand through the wire and wrung that little bastard's neck, like a chicken. *Figlio di puttana!*" Nonno twisted his fists together in a swift, excited parody of the execution. "Tasted better than chicken though." His head strained back on his brittle neck, his laugh bubbling over into a shuddering hack. Pipo, in his kennel by the *forno* whimpered at the sound of him. Examining his expectorations in the dirt, Nonno rumbled, "*Si*, I've had a dog, *porco Dio*. It wasn't mine, but I've had one." He rattled up the steps to the house, his charcoal and piss scent hanging behind him in the thick night air.

Uncle Vinny put his arm around her. "It's different for their generation, Caroli'. They had to survive, you see?" But all she could think of was how to save her dog.

"What happened to Rondinella, *Zio*?"

Uncle Vinny turned to look at Pipo watching them though his eyelashes, intently, perhaps sensing his life depended on it. "It's a long time ago now." He exhaled to the bottom of his lungs as if the memory was buried down there somewhere in the sediment of the past, reluctant to be disturbed.

"*Zio?*"

"Well … after the war Nonno was eventually shipped back to Italy. Rondinella was knocking on a bit by then, probably on her last legs anyway. Besides, the next year your granddad packed us all up to leave for our new life in England."

"But what did he *do* to her?" she insisted, her eyes alight with realization.

Uncle Vinny rubbed at his damp neck and looked back again at Pipo. "We lost all our chickens one night. Scattered round the coop, their necks broken every one of them, as if for the fun of it. Nonno blamed Rondinella. I never saw her again. Your granddad said she'd run off and probably been bitten by one of the rabid wolves in the Lupini hills. I looked everywhere for her … I searched, you know …" He looked up as if asking for forgiveness and then turned away. "Like I said, she was old …"

He'd told enough for both of them. They sat quietly in the night, listening to the scratch of crickets in their throats and the strangled complaints of a donkey in the valley.

In the last week of that summer, they came back from the beach at Nettuno and found Pipo laid out in a pool of blood that was curdling down the chalk road. Nonno was leaning on a spade. "Donati's truck reversing up the Colle Lungo smashed his head like a ripe tomato. *Madonna!*" He slammed a sandpaper palm against the spade handle, his lifeless skin chaffing the old wood. After a while he said, "It was quick, though. Vincenz', dig a hole in the long grass down the hill." But as he handed the spade to Uncle Vinny, Carolina saw the blood on its blade and the upturned pots of basil on the verandah steps.

The summer she turned sixteen, Nonno floated in waves of purple satin, wearing his wedding suit and a smile she had never seen him wear in life. A few brittle veterans tottered over the cobbles behind the coffin, smelling of mothballs, heads held high in the starched collars of their original *camicie nere*. Women hung with black lace wailed in operatic vibrato in the church aisles. At the wake a man with no teeth and only one eye pinned her fingertips between his parchment hands and told her that her grandfather had delivered him from death. She smiled stiffly and nodded, searching for the familiar comfort of Uncle Vinny in the awkward foreignness of it all. The one-eyed man had been a prisoner with Nonno in Tobruk, Uncle Vinny explained. "Thirty thousand of them penned into a square of barbed wire mesh, he says. Like animals, only not fed as often. He says they fought each other for food, even scavenged among the dead. The old boy reckons Nonno could make shit edible." The one-eyed man nodded gravely, then absently shuffled away.

"Like dogs," she heard him mumbling to anyone who would listen. "Like dogs ..."

Before the coffin was sealed, Carolina lined up with her family for the farewell kiss. She looked down at her grandfather, trying to see his living face, but all she saw was his skin glowing pearly gray and she thought of the full moon and wolves howling in the Lupini hills. She bent to kiss his cheek but stopped and pressed her lips to the wood of his rosary instead. After all, she had never seen a dead person before. You don't get up close to death in East Anglia. The only dead thing she had ever seen was her dog Pipo.

Mr. Potato Head

By Sally Quilford

One morning, Madge Harris got up out of bed and found that her husband had turned into a potato. She knew it was George as the potato was in sitting in his chair, facing the television. It was his favourite place to be as he shouted orders.

"Get my tea, Madge."

"Fetch the biscuits, Madge."

"Madge, turn that bloody fire down! My legs are burning."

Any tardiness on Madge's part was repaid with the sting of his slipper on bare skin.

Madge picked up the potato and placed a cushion underneath, so that it - George would have a better view of the television. His few strands of remaining hair manifested themselves in tiny stalks at the top of his head. Unfortunately the transformation had only left him with the one eye and that was quite low down on his body. Madge did consider turning him upside down, but thought better of it. It occurred to her that it might be his naval.

It was pleasant for the first few days. She'd sit there in the evenings, sewing and watching him watching television. Not much different to their normal life, except she didn't have to jump up every five minutes. That began to pall, not least because George was starting to age rapidly. She supposed she ought to find a way to bring him back to normal.

"A potato, you say?" said Doctor Kumar, his eyes twinkling. "I always did tell George that if he didn't get moving, he'd turn into a couch potato."

"So that's it, then," said Madge. "Your prophecy came true. There must be a way to bring him back. Antibiotics? A tonic?"

"A nice gravy?" said Kumar. "I tell you what, Mrs Harris. I'll write you a prescription. But I want you to take these. Then, when George … returns, let me know and I'll see what I can do for him."

It wasn't the answer Madge was looking for. Why should she take tablets for George's affliction? She returned home and switched on the television.

"Has your partner changed recently?" asked Trisha. "Has it made life unbearable for you? Call me on this number and I'll give you the help you need."

Whilst Madge wouldn't have said life was unbearable – George didn't usually let her watch daytime chat shows – she did think she should do the best for him.

Going to the studio was very nice. They put her up in a hotel overnight then made her up to look quite pretty, and loaned her a nice dress to wear. They even buffed George up, though the make-up girl was a bit too rough and knocked off one of his stalks.

"Do be careful," said Madge. "He's very particular about his hair."

"Oh, okay," said the girl. "Sorry, Mr Harris."

"Today," Trisha told the audience, "We bring you the story of the man who turned into a potato. First we'll speak to his wife. Hello, Madge. Tell us about George."

Madge told her story, after which George was carried out on a throne-like chair. They'd put a little crown on his head.

"George, tell me, why have you put your wife through this?" asked Trisha. George didn't answer. "I don't know about you people in the audience, but think his silence says it all."

"He won't speak because you've made him look ridiculous!" said Madge.

Madge went home, dejected, but the following day she received offers to appear on *GMTV*, *This Morning* and *Richard and Judy*. As they all offered to put her and George up in posh hotels, she accepted, enjoying the trappings of celebrity. A famous hypnotist tried to put George in a trance, but conceded it was difficult dealing with someone with only one eye. Jeremy Kyle told George to "get a job'.

Then the newspapers told her story, including one called *The Sport*, who for some reason wanted a picture of Madge without her top. As George didn't seem to mind and they offered her a lot of money, she agreed. When she saw the proof pictures, she had to admit she looked quite nice, whilst her husband, in the background, looked very drab and boring.

"You might make more of an effort," she told him on the way home. "Your hair is getting terribly long."

She hardly knew what to do with all the money in the bank. It was something that George always handled, giving her just enough to do the shopping every week. Even after spending money on new clothes for her television appearances, she had cash to spare.

"Would it be so awful if I went away on holiday?" she asked George one night. "I could ask someone to take care of you. My new best friend, Abi Titmuss, might do it. She's a sweet girl. A nurse. I think you'd like her." She took his silence as a yes. "I could take you with me but ..." It would be too unkind to tell him that he cramped her style.

In the end, Madge left George to fend for himself. It wasn't as if he needed much looking after. He didn't eat or drink, and had no real need of clothes. "You really should drink," she'd told him, worried about how dry his skin was becoming.

She went to America, and that was where she met Jake. She had no illusions. Jake was a beach bum, looking for a rich woman to fleece. He gave her sex and she paid him back with a new surfboard or, after a particularly good night, a jet ski.

"Madge," Jake said to her one night. He lay naked, face down on her bed. A blush, the shape of Madge's flip flop, was just beginning to fade on his bare buttock. "Honey, I know what I am. I'm a beach bum and a gigolo. But I am honest about it. Which is why I'm going to say this about George. Isn't it possible that he just up and left?"

Madge thought about it for a moment. "That's strange," she said. "Richard Madeley didn't think of that, and he's usually quite good at these things."

"No one else has suggested it?"

"No." She lay awake, thinking about it all, remembering Doctor Kumar offering her tablets that she thought should have been for George. What if George had just left and, after thirty years of doing his dirty work, she couldn't accept it? But George wouldn't leave. Or if he did, he'd have insisted on her packing his bags and carrying them to the station for him. Probably got her unpacking them at the other end too. Unless...

"He never really went anywhere to meet another woman," Madge said to Jake some time later. "And it doesn't explain the potato."

"Maybe he was peeling some then decided to go."

"George? Peel a potato!" She laughed until she cried, the humour becoming a deep, deep sadness. Jake held her, soothed her.

"It's okay, Madge," he said. "Let it all out."

Two weeks later she kissed Jake goodbye, and returned home. As she walked up the garden path, she had a feeling of things being different. No, not different. Back to normal. She unlocked the door and went into the sitting room.

"Where've you been?" He was sitting in his usual chair by the fire, his spud-u-like head glistening with sweat. The bossy, bullying, boring George on whom she'd wasted thirty years.

"I might ask you the same question, George."

"Mind your own business." Madge wondered if he knew. "Get me a cup of tea and tell me what the fuck this is all about." He held up a paper in one hand, his slipper in the other. Emblazoned on the front page was Madge, topless. Even allowing for the awkwardness of the situation she still thought she looked quite good for her age.

"Mind *your* own business and get your own cup of tea, Mr Potato Head," said Madge. She turned around and left the way she came.

The Aquarium

(Honorable Mention)

By Josh McDonald

Sometimes we are fishes and we wiggle up and down on the floor. My shorts hurt when we do that because there is a string that goes inside to hold them up and it presses on my bones. My hip bones. "Your knee bone connected to your thigh bone. Your thigh bone connected to you hip bone. Hear the word of the Lord." And then you shake your hands at the ceiling and then you wiggle all the different bits. You do that standing up. But when you're pretending to be fishes you swim on the floor, but it's not swimming it's dancing. Dad says it's dancing but it's swimming but it's dancing. It used to be a swimming pool but then they put a floor over the swimming pool and they made it dancing. But they've still got tiles at the side with grips so your toes can hold it. But the changing rooms don't smell of feet and chlorine. They just smell a bit of feet and paint. Because they're always painting and they never finish painting. They should finish painting and then they wouldn't need to paint anymore. Once I tried to do a back flip off the side at a real swimming pool where they have double size aero chocolate and I hit my head on the side but I was ok because I didn't crack my skull but if I did crack my skull I might have died but once I won the under 9's cubs backstroke and wotsit with the sideburns gave me a certificate and I was cold but they let you take towels into swimming.

But you can't take towels into dancing, you can only take shorts and a vest and one jumper and you have to ask to go to the toilet so you can't pee in the water like at Stokewood Road baths. But one girl did once. She peed on the floor and we all had to stop and her mother had to come and get her because she cried and I got a drink out of the drink machine without paying because I found a stick you could poke in and no one was watching but it was Diet Coke and I hate Diet Coke because it doesn't taste as good and when we started dancing I really wanted to pee but I thought Mrs Jacobs would be angry because we'd hardly done any dancing because of the girl that peed on the floor so I kept it in but when Dad came I was bursting so we had so stop on the way home to pee and Dad was embarrassed because he told me off for sniffing snot up my nose all the time but he told me in a loud way and normally he's quiet except when the bills come and then there's no fucking way they're charging that much for one bit of pipe for fucksake.

But sometimes we're not fish, we're rays. Last time we saw the video it had a ray in it which is like a squashed shark or a pancake when you put the golden syrup in and fold it in half and put the brown sugar on top from the white bowl with the man on it. And when you swim like a ray you go on your front and you move your bum and put your hands out wide like you're flying and if you are able to you put your head up. Next week we're going to be sharks because I asked specially and we're doing a piece at the end of term called the sea and we're all bits of the sea but we haven't done sharks yet which is basically a shame because they have the most teeth and they can sniff blood through their nose.

Mrs Jacobs has a nose like a shark. Basically it's all pointy like an aeroplane but I don't think she likes sharks at all. Because when everyone else was being a starfish I pretended to be a shark and eat off Toby's leg and he told me to go do myself in and hit me on the arm but I told him to hit me on the nose because that is where sharks sniff best and it kills them to be punched on it. But Mrs Jacobs told me off and said we're doing sharks next week which I think basically is unfair because starfish are like greens or having to go on walks. But I like Mrs Jacobs because sometimes she rubs my hair after she moves my arms about but sometimes she needs to use more deodorant which I told dad but he said don't be personal and then he showed me my pants with skid marks in.

Starfish can grow their legs back and that's why I thought Toby wouldn't mind if I bit his off but I had to go and lie next to Kylie and there's no point eating her because she's got stupid hair. And it was when we were on our backs being starfish stretching out our legs and doing quiet time that I saw Mum in the ceiling. She was far away in the window in the top part of the ceiling but she was looking at me and smiling and saying brush your hair but she knew I couldn't brush my hair because I was a starfish and it was quiet time. She had her hands pressed down on the glass like she had landed and I wondered if she had got there after a fall. And my brain was saying I was a durr because it was impossible but basically I was happy because it had been a long time, years, but I was also sad and I cried without opening my mouth and then we had to go and get our shoes and go into main reception but I stayed there on the floor looking up until Mrs Jacobs told me to go and when Dad came to collect me I didn't tell him but in the car on the way back I told him that Mum was in the ceiling and she had fallen there and at first he didn't say anything but the top of his head went into lines and he bit his lip but then he said that Mum wasn't here anymore and I knew that and that she was gone but I said I saw her in the ceiling and she told me to brush my hair and I had to read her lips to tell what she was saying. And then Dad stopped the car and said wait there and went into the twenty four hour Spar and didn't come out for ages and when he did his eyes were red and he had scrape marks on his cheeks. And then he said do you want to see a film and I said yes because I can have one popcorn or one chocolate but not both and I can have a bath before but not after as there isn't time basically. And we didn't talk any more and all the sounds in the car were louder and the windscreen wipers squeaked like the white board at school when the pens have run out and the only one left is the red one but you can't use the red one and no one says why.

Today I'm a shark. I'm the only one. All the boys and Daisy wanted to be a shark but then we all started eating each other and tearing off each others heads with the millions of teeth and there was loads of blood and Mrs Jacobs said there were too many sharks and so that I would be the only shark for the time being but not anyone else for the time being because I had asked specially but I could only be a shark if I didn't eat anyone for the time being. So for the time being I am not eating anyone and I am swimming between the jelly fish and the seaweed and the rays and the oysters and the crabs and the octopus and I am sniffing for blood and showing my teeth that I brush with fluoride stripes with blood bits in them and I am the biggest of the sea and if anyone tries to do me in then I will do them all over and pull them down and eat them in my cave with my teeth that can cut and knife up. Swoosh, swoosh, swoosh, sniff, sniff, sniff. Toby has a plaster on his leg. I sniff it for blood and he does me on the nose but Mrs Jacobs doesn't see so I tell him he's a wankstain and he knows how dangerous I am even though I'm not going to eat anyone for the time being and then I'm off swimming faster than anyone else and they all whizz past like the people outside when I'm in the car going to school all squashed and blurred up like when you press your eyeball in at people. And when I'm in the car I'm a shark and all the people are bits that I can bite off so the bits fall into bits and no one can do anything about it because I am a shark and I can swim faster than anybody. My teeth have got bits of blood in it and Mrs Jacobs pats me on the head and says its quiet time now and I lie on my back like a starfish with everyone else and we do stretches and Mum is there in the window in the ceiling with her hands pressed against the glass. And she asks me if I've been good and I say yes and then I wonder if she heard me say wankstain and I say I'm sorry I'm really sorry I'm really really sorry and she smiles at me and I tell her I'm not eating anyone and she laughs and I cry without making a noise because its quiet time but the more I try and stop crying I do it more and I'm afraid everyone will hear and I am a shark and I am the biggest in the sea and I can swim faster than anyone and mum says don't worry don't worry and her hands move up and down on the glass like she is moving her hand up and down on me and I can't properly feel her but I sort of can and I stop crying but I've got loads of snot over my lips and it tastes like blood.

And then Mrs Jacobs says its time to go and I'm the only one lying on the floor and so I get up and I wipe my nose and Mrs Jacobs talks with my Dad after everyone else has left and I sit on the bench with my jumper on my knees while she talks and I'm shaking a bit and Dad puts my jumper on and carries me to the car and then we drive off and I tell him I saw Mum in the ceiling and he says it's OK and then he says we'll have baked beans when we get home and then he stops the car and says Mum really loved you you know that don't you and I say yes and then I don't say anything and neither does he and we drive home slowly so I can see the faces of the people outside and each one is different and I don't want to eat baked beans I just want to lie in bed and close my eyes and be still for such a long time it feels like forever.

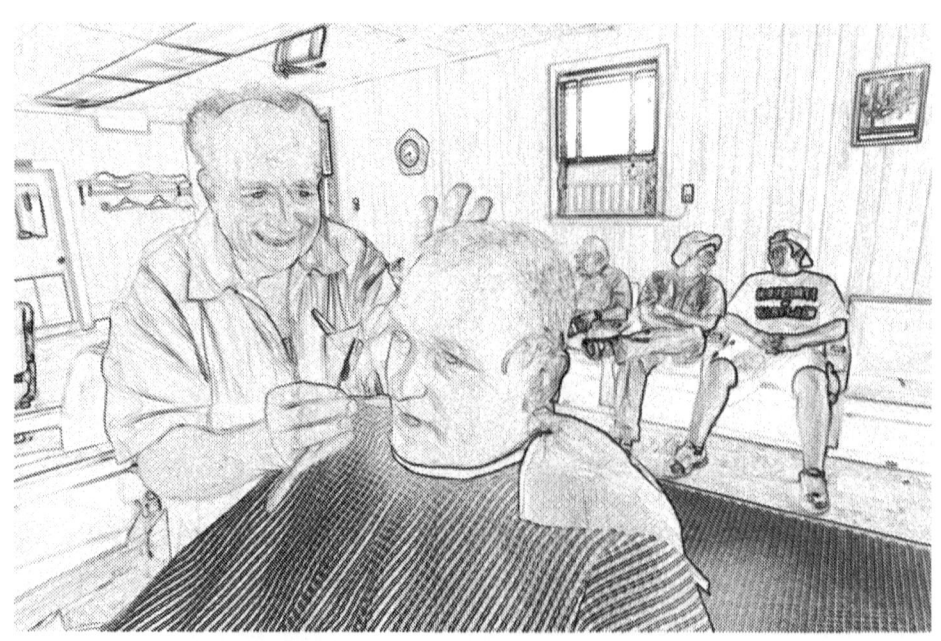

Crazy

(Honorable Mention)

By Swathi Kappagantula

Pichamma, they called her in the village. The crazy one. She was far from raving, like the real crazies who wandered about with wild hair and vacant looks. In fact, her keen sense of domestic service and duty was central to the efficient functioning of most Brahmin households in the community. Nevertheless, all the villagers had called her Pichamma for as long as Ramu could remember.

He knew Pichamma was not old, but Ramu found it difficult to compare her with the women of his family because of her weathered skin and shaven head and worn cotton sarees. She was a tall and sinewy woman, and at times Ramu suspected that the women's avoidance of Pichamma appeared more deferential than disdainful.

Ramu was one of the youngest, and when school was closed he had little to do but follow Pichamma around on her various rounds. The women of the house sometimes sent him on an errand to request or deliver information to other families. An impromptu cricket game was usually struck late in the afternoon. But Ramu took his daily duties with Pichamma seriously, warning older Brahmin women of Pichamma's approach so they could avert their eyes if they had not yet eaten or performed daily prayers.

Ramu would be Pichamma's advance party, announcing to each household her arrival so she could clean and scrub all the rooms (except the prayer rooms and kitchens, just the kitchen floors) without too much disruption. He believed himself to have the valuable role of village sentry, and shouted "Pichamma is here!" with arms crossed and skinny legs blocking each threshold, until the coast was clear.

Ramu's own house was particularly difficult to monitor, with five Brahmin women living under one roof. Ramu's grandmother was careful in her avoidance of Pichamma, with the daughters-in-law taking a slightly more relaxed approach to the servant who was the same age as some of them. With her stubbly head bent, Pichamma would clean as the younger women picked up their sewing or books and moved to another part of the house, with the exception of Saroja, his mother.

In his house, Ramu's mother was practically the only person who interacted with Pichamma. The bulk of the domestic management fell on his mother's shoulders, not only as the youngest daughter-in-law but as a widow with 11 children dependent on the household resources. Ramu's father had died the previous year of diphtheria, leaving his mother at the relative mercy of an extended family that was typically Brahminic in both its religious and financial austerity. His uncles and aunts regretfully agreed amongst themselves that the care of 11 children should be shared between various relatives' in nearby villages and towns.

Ramu's mother waged a constant and quiet battle against hints at such dispersion, succumbing only to suggestions that her oldest daughter could be married as soon as she turned 16. Thus, Pichamma's duties to Saroja went beyond routine housecleaning and organization, to include the passing on of information regarding overheard plans to send Ramu's brothers to work in the town or news of an eligible bachelor in a neighboring village. Pichamma whispered, head bent as she squatted and scampered about the floor with a rag or broom, while Saroja sat staring into a book. Often, still staring into the unread book, his mother would cry as Pichamma moved around the room.

Ramu always stood guard at these moments, unsure of whether his aunts would be more horrified at encountering Pichamma before prayer time or at witnessing his mother's emotional display in front of a servant.

As it was, his mother and siblings were the subject of much debate amongst his uncles and aunts.

"Saroja is a good woman, but she is terribly unlucky."

"What a pity to outlive your husband, and that too with 11 children."

"Are we expected to feed them, educate them, and marry them off as well?"

"If the older boys worked in the city, they could at least send some money home."

Ramu realized that despite such simmering resentments, the treatment that Saroja received was not that bad. After his father had died, his uncles and aunts had discussed the fact that now, after Independence, it was not necessary to insist that Saroja shave her head if she did not want to do so voluntarily. She had shiny, black, waist-length hair that Ramu loved to comb and braid. He was thrilled when she announced that she would not shave her head, and that her dead husband who had been a progressive thinker would have been proud of her decision.

Saroja continued to wear her jewelry as well, unlike his grandmother, and Ramu always marveled at the way her diamond earrings and gold chains would sparkle in the sun when she walked outside. They sparkled this way on the afternoon she waved him back to the house as he followed her down the dirt road that led into the village, saying she had to go discuss something with someone and that it was no place for a little boy.

Ramu returned to the house, went around to the side, and squatted with his chin in his hands to watch the older boys at their game of cricket. He could watch them for hours, and it was nearly dark when he heard voices gathering in front of their house.

"Where could she have gone? When did she leave?"

"It's been almost four hours! Eh, Ramu, when did you last see your mother?"

"I don't know, right before Subbu scored his first run."

"Stupid fool, no time sense. What's the use of asking him?"

The adults continued to argue amongst themselves, and Ramu backed up until he was flat against the whitewashed wall of the house. He realized, looking around with confused then fearful eyes, that they could not find his mother. As evening progressed, Ramu stayed flattened against the wall, wishing he could become a part of it and not have to witness the men leaving with lit torches to begin searching the fields, or the women sitting on their cots shaking their heads and talking about his unfortunate parents.

When a group of men walked over to the well with a torch to illuminate what or who might be at the bottom, Ramu turned to face the wall and pushed his face into it until he heard his nose make a faint cracking sound. But eventually he heard them drag the cover back over the well and go off to search elsewhere.

It was then that his oldest aunt came over and gently peeled him off the wall, now stained with tears. She took him to a cot on one side of the verandah, and made him sit in her lap.

"Don't worry, Ramu, we will find her. She will return soon."

"Return from where? Where did she go? She told me she had to talk to someone."

"Sometimes it is frustrating for your mother to be without a husband."

"Many people don't have husbands. Many women, like Grandmother, and Pichamma. They do not go away."

"Your Grandfather died a long time ago, and she has grown accustomed to living without him. It was before you were born, that is why her head is shaven."

"Is that why Pichamma's head is shaven?"

"That is a different story."

"Please tell me the story, I want to hear a story."

And Ramu's aunt began to tell him a story of a young servant woman named Sampathu, who had been married to a man from this village and moved here when she was 17. Sampathu was from a poor family of servants, and was married off to the only match that would take her for no dowry at her advanced age. She was strong and quick-witted, and quickly became a sought-after servant in many of the households in the village.

Sampathu bore two children, working until the day each child was born and returning to her duties within days of giving birth. This commitment to her work was partly motivated by the fact that her husband could not hold any steady employment, and could usually be found lying on a cot outside their hut in a fog of *bhang* and bootleg liquor.

One day, Sampathu came home to find the older child cut and bleeding, having fallen while toddling, and the baby screaming in her soiled blankets. The husband was nowhere to be found, and did not return that night or for many, many nights after that one. Sampathu began bringing her children to the homes where she worked, and continued until they could easily be left with another woman for a few hours.

A year later, Sampathu's husband reappeared, begging her forgiveness and saying that he had gone away to change his ways. But after a few weeks of odd jobs, he would somehow find his former spot on his old cot, and at night in his drunken rage he would beat her.

For years this continued, with Sampathu working to send her two children to the local school and her husband reappearing and disappearing. Until one day when he returned, already drunk this time, and Sampathu locked the gate that she had had built during the previous year, her hut having turned into a much improved shack with a tin roof. The drunk husband could not for all his rage manage to unlock this new gate, and began screaming until a crowd of villagers gathered outside Sampathu's shack.

The children were at school, and her husband began to cause such a commotion that people could not help but become involved.

"Why will she not open the gate? This is her husband after all, drunk or not."

"That useless village idiot, he was lucky to get her in the first place."

"Eh, Sampathu, open the gate, this is too much disturbance, I say."

Eventually, Sampathu emerged from the shack. She began shouting at her husband, and at the chorus of villagers.

"Leave me in peace! All of you, go and leave me in peace!"

But the arguing continued, with her husband shouting and cursing at her, the gate, and the growing crowd of bystanders. Sampathu emerged from the shack again, this time holding a small steel bowl full of water. She went back inside, and came out again with soap and rag, and once again with a small handmirror and a blade.

Sampathu leaned the mirror against a rock, and crossed her legs to sit in front of it with the bowl of water beside her. The crowd gasped as she began, with the mid-day sun reflecting off of her black braid as she unraveled it, to hack at her long, thick hair.

"She has gone mad, the woman has gone crazy, that is why she won't unlock the gate you see!" shouted her husband.

"Definitely crazy."

"No doubt."

Sampathu continued her slow and mechanical hacking until all around her in the dry dirt was a round blanket of black hair. Left on her head were tufts a few inches long, which she moistened with the water from the bowl and some soap. And then, to the utter horror of the crowd that grown to include almost all the villagers, she proceeded, carefully and slowly, to shave her head.

Nobody shouted any longer, deciding that it was futile to reason with a madwoman. But people continued to stare, wondering what the outcome of this incredible drama would be – nobody had ever seen anything like this.

Finally, with her head cleanly shaven, Sampathu stood and patted her exposed scalp, glistening in the sun, with the end of her saree. She had cut herself a few times, but it was nothing serious. Nothing as serious as the damage she had done to her reputation, with this mad behaviour that could never have been imagined.

Sampathu approached the gate, and looked straight at her husband.

"You are dead to me. I no longer have a husband, and now everyone knows that you are dead to me."

And then, an even more incredible thing happened. Nobody argued with her. After she spoke, people started retreating to their homes. Not one person uttered a sound, not even her husband. Sampathu went back inside her shack, and he was never seen in the village again. From that day onwards, although she continued to clean houses and work, nobody called her Sampathu. She came to be known as Pichamma.

Ramu sat in his aunt's lap, clinging onto her as he imagined this final scene in front of Pichamma's shack. He fell asleep like this, his mind racing through a tumbled confusion of loyalty and disgust and wonderment and then fear, as he remembered that his mother was still missing.

In the morning, Ramu woke on his cot to the sound of his uncles and aunts arguing in the main room. He then remembered his missing mother, and his dry mouth suddenly felt completely parched.

Ramu got out of bed and slowly walked to the main room, fearful of learning that his mother had been found at the bottom of the well or on the train tracks at the edge of town or on the riverbank. His mind raced with these images of his helpless mother stranded with no one to help her, but as he approached his uncles and aunts he overheard a combination of relief and irritation.

"How could she have just left, without telling anyone? What does she think?"

"Leaving all those children? Is she crazy? What would we have done with them?"

"It is your job to keep an eye on her now, this is too much tension."

"So insensitive, so selfish. My head is killing me from the stress."

Ramu turned and walked towards his mother's room, where he used to find his parents lying together early in the mornings when he could not sleep. From the doorway, he saw Pichamma sweeping the floor with her bundle of straw. He saw his mother on her bed, weeping openly, with no book in her hand. And when Pichamma began sweeping the small pile of dust toward the threshold where he stood, Ramu saw that she too wept.

Ramu turned and walked away, not wanting to be in the presence of a grief that he could not share. He went to the verandah and stood outside the front door of the house, arms crossed and squinting into the bright morning sunlight. He, like everyone else, was just relieved that his mother was home.

Epiphany

By Lucy Palmer

Once Martin and the girls, and their new roller blades, had gone Marion took the Christmas decorations box back out from the cupboard under the stairs.

The branches of the Christmas tree were drooping as though all the sap had gone out of them, and now and then there was a dry patter of falling needles. Marion opened up the battered cardboard box and methodically laid out the smaller boxes in rows, like so many little coffins she thought. She began unhooking the baubles, her favorites and the most fragile: bright drops of crimson and emerald, ultramarine, silver, gold. She placed them one by one in their cotton wool hollows, like gaudy eggs. They reassured her, neatly nestled in their boxes, full of the promise of next year, but every year there were more and more empty spaces. Last year she had even had to throw one box away because there were not enough baubles left to fill it. Turning back to the tree, Marion saw that this year, yet again, one branch had sagged so low that its bauble had slid off and dropped to the ground. It was cracked, and one side splintered into fragments as she picked it up. The glass seemed impossibly thin: such a fragile shell against the emptiness without and the emptiness within.

Next, she removed the little cherubs. They made the tips of her fingers sparkle. In some places the naked plastic was starting to show through the glitter, and over the years a layer of twinkling silt was being deposited in the corners of the box. The wooden figures were holding up a little better. One angel had lost a wing, but at least from one side it looked complete, and one of the wise men had lost his gift. Marion was sure that they had all borne offerings last year, and looked at the other two to see what they held. The first, clothed in blue, wore a golden crown on his brown hair and in his proffered hands was a shining ingot. That was Melchior, bearing gold. The second was dressed in crimson robes and matching turban. He had a tumbling white beard that fell to his waist and his skin was pale. He was carrying a box or casket, so he must be Caspar bringing frankincense. The king with the empty hands was dark-skinned and was wearing green. Of course, that was Balthazar and the missing gift was myrrh. Marion bent down and sifted through the fallen needles in the hope of finding the phial. The needles stuck into her jumper and pricked her skin, but there was no sign of the missing gift.

Marion gave it up and began taking off the other decorations: stars and bells and icicles and stockings. She had always found it sad that the stockings were so flat and empty; that there were so clearly no presents inside. She thought, unhappily, of Alice.

All the decorations that had hung on the tree were now removed and lay in their little coffins. In the pale light of the January morning they looked somewhat tawdry, the gorgeous regalia of Christmas Eve reduced to tatty trinkets.

The tinsel was also looking a bit sparse. It reminded Marion, humorlessly, of Martin's hair. Last of all she unwound the fairy lights and the tree stood naked, bereft of all its gewgaws, looking shabby and forlorn. Sitting on the floor beside the decorations, Marion looked forlornly back at it. She always removed the decorations on her own; made sure the children were not around, to spare them the disenchantment. They were probably old enough now not to be upset, but she continued to undress the tree alone. Yes, they were a bit too old now to get really excited about Christmas. Last year Emily had no longer wanted to help decorate the tree and this year Alice had finally realized, on Christmas Eve itself, that Santa did not exist.

"I knew it," she had crowed gleefully, triumphant at having acceded at last to the sphere of adult rationality "I knew it!" She, Marion, had been devastated. At the end of the evening she had lingered downstairs, washing up, until she was sure that Martin would be asleep, and then had sobbed silently into her pillow until she could cry no more

That Christmas Eve, for the first time in several years, they had had Carl and Jenny over for mulled wine and carols. Jenny did not seem to have forgotten how to play the piano accompaniments, but Marion had found that she could no longer reach the descant part of *Oh Come All Ye Faithful*. The pain of Alice's discovery seemed to constrict her throat and make it difficult to breathe.

In the end, Christmas Day had come and gone uneventfully. Martin's mother had arrived more or less on time and, for once, had not stayed too late. The girls had been satisfied with their presents. Marion had produced the perfect turkey with all the trimmings. She herself had not eaten much. Something about the permission for excess made her lose her appetite.

Carl and Jenny had been back for New Year's Eve, along with Alan and Sarah. Flamboyant Alan with his Mediterranean good looks; elegant Sarah, so insightful and self-contained; Carl the cynical intellectual; pretty pre-Raphaelite Jenny with her pale complexion and long dark hair – they were still Martin's friends really, although they had known each other so long. A certain wary politeness separated the women. They would exchange cordial compliments on children, jewelry or cooking, but rarely anything more intimate.

The meal, Sarah had commented, was delicious: festive but not too heavy although, with her usual self-restraint, she had drunk and eaten little. Marion noticed with guilty satisfaction that Sarah was perhaps not quite as perfectly sculpted as she had been in the past: her cheeks seemed a little fuller and there was a hint of puffiness under the eyes. As for Jenny, she was as slim as ever. Her face appeared slightly drawn, perhaps, in repose, but she was in almost constant animation, laughing gaily and tossing her head, sending waves through her thick dark hair, gesticulating with her long jeweled fingers. She was playing up the effects of the wine, Marion thought, watching the pretty head lolling on the slender hand and arm.

Emily and Anaïs, Carl and Jenny's daughter, had drunk a glass of wine each and pleaded to be allowed to stay up with the adults. Edwin, Alan and Sarah's youngest had complained of stomach ache then vomited in the toilet. Alice had taken several sips from her sister's glass and had cavorted wildly round the room until Martin made all the children go to bed.

With and without the children, they had played word games after the meal: Pictionary for the children, Taboo and Chicanery for the adults. Martin was by far the best at them; they were, as Carl had commented, his games. It was odd, Marion thought, how he should be so gifted with words in the abstract and how he should use them so sparingly, almost disdainfully, in relation to everyday life. Words were for Martin theoretical a discipline like pure maths or logic. For Alan they were a mirror for his own brilliance and for Carl a weapon against perceived artifice. For herself, Marion suspected, words were none of these things.

She had tried to enjoy herself, though, she really had. Perhaps a little too hard, had laughed a little too much, too merrily, but without ever quite achieving the satisfaction of being drunk. She had begun to feel more and more detached from the conversation; it was as if something had imperceptibly shifted. It was not the distance of vagueness. There was no trace of haze. On the contrary, everything had focused into unbearable clarity as though something inside had glassed over a splinter from the Snow Queen's mirror, or Plath's bell jar. The bawdy jokes ceased to be funny but were merely facetious or crude. The clever deconstruction of the Queen's speech no longer seemed witty. It was just so much intellectual strutting and preening. She imagined Alan in his garish waistcoat as a puffed-up cock-pheasant, bright eye darting, beak ever poised to peck. The thought irritated rather than amused her. She could not keep up the laughter; no longer felt any compulsion to respond. The invisible barrier before her acted like a magnifying glass, revealing coarseness and pockmarks of character with a scientific precision that she found appalling.

After some time – Marion had no idea how long – Sarah came graciously over to her and laid a gentle hand on her forearm. It took all Marion's self-control to keep from snatching it away.

"You must be getting tired," said Sarah with a benevolence that sounded to Marion forced and patronizing. Not trusting herself to answer civilly, she merely nodded silently and waited for the evening, and the next day's breakfast, to be over.

And now it was all over. Christmas, New Year and Epiphany over for another year. The decorations were almost all packed away. The tree stood drooping and bare. Marion picked up the figures of the wise men and laid them gently in their box. There was still no sign of the missing myrrh: the eastern king was still without a present. She was reminded of T.S. Eliot's *O Journey of the Magi*. They had studied it at school, had even learnt it by heart, and despite all the textual analysis it had meant nothing to her, but now, all of a sudden, the words struck her as intensely meaningful: all that journey, all that tiresome effort and what for, when it came down to it? What for? For a new beginning that was the augury of an ending, of loss, of estrangement and of sorrow. Would she do it again, she wondered. She did not know. Wearily, Marion closed the lid on the decorations.

"I should be glad," she murmured, "of another death," and put the box back into the cupboard.

Cry Baby

(Honorable Mention)

By Catherine Binnie

The neon light of the credit card pin machine blinked slowly "checking card...please wait... checking card..." Emma tried to focus on a point above the till, whilst the shop assistant, oblivious to the shots of panic running down Emma's spine, flapped open a carrier bag and began to pack the shopping – six DVDs, two pairs of shoes, pink tracksuit trousers with a matching t-shirt emblazoned with the word "angel', the same outfit again – this time in powder blue, and a face paint kit. Also, for the bag, the whole purpose of the visit – Benji The Bear (He talks! He sings! He dances!). The one item she had planned to pick up and leave, ignoring the rows of sparkling pink plastic and the inevitable accompanying pleas. He was a replacement for Robbie the Rabbit, whose happy songs about daisy picking had been forever silenced following a run-in with the cat. Secretly, Emma understood the animal's feelings about Robbie, but Lily had been inconsolable. A trip to Toyworld and the discovery of Benji had dissolved her daughter's crumpled frown and soothed her red, dripping nose. Emma found herself grinding her teeth in annoyance at the thought of Lily's tears – despite "The Bear', she knew it wouldn't be long before some other horror would distract her and the crying and clinging and hiccoughed exclaims of "Mummy!" would start again. She glanced at her daughter, who, apart from the occasional sniff had forgotten about the traumas of the morning and was now absorbed with stretching and flexing the limbs of her Barbie doll.

"Lily!" Emma's voice was sharp, "stop sniffing"

Lily sniffed and turned her face to her mother, eyes wet.

"Don't even think about it," she hissed.

The shop assistant glanced up from her packing, and caught Lily's eye with a smile and a wink. Lily squirmed with delight.

Emma gave the assistant a hard stare, "It's called discipline."

The assistant returned her stare blankly.

"It is important to have control of your child."

The assistant gave a half shrug and returned to the packing, an imperceptible smile on her face. The till chuntered into life, and with a leaden lurch of the stomach Emma knew what was coming.

"It's saying card not accepted. Do you have another one?"

There was a shuffle of interest in the queue, leaning in at the hint of a drama unfolding. Emma felt the back of her neck burn as she rifled through her bag, the pretence that she had another seemed necessary.

She smiled, "I must have left it at home"

"Mummy," Lily tugged at her sleeve.

"Well, what do you want me to do with these?" the assistant indicated to the mound of bags.

"Mummy!" Lily's voice stretched to a whine, as she sensed that Benji might not be coming home with them. Emma ignored her and turned back to the assistant, "I'll come back for them later"

"How much later? We only keep things for an hour you know"

A tutting swept the queue, Emma could feel the stares blanketing her back.

"Mummyyyyy!" the tugging became more persistent. Emma snapped her arm out of her daughter's reach. Lily stepped back, startled, and sucked her breath, ready for a wail. Emma grabbed the hood of Lily's coat and yanked her towards the door, ignoring her loud, protesting squawks. Once outside and around the corner, hidden from the stares of other customers gratified by this burst of misbehavior, Emma knelt, face to face with her daughter.

"You will stop crying" she said in a fierce whisper.

A fat tear rolled down Lily's cheek. Emma stopped herself from wiping it away. That was no way to learn.

"I have told you before. No-one likes a cry baby. You carry on like that and nobody will want to be your friend." The tears continued to run and Lily ran her tongue along her lips catching each one in turn. She showed no sign of understanding, or even hearing, her mother's words. Typical. There was only one language her daughter understood.

"You will stop this very second or that's it, Barbie will go in the bin". Lily squeaked in distress and clasped Barbie to her chest.

"Understood?" Emma asked.

Lily nodded and stretched her arms out for sign that she was forgiven. Emma gave her a blank smile.

"Naughty girls don't get hugs do they?"

Her daughter's face fell, but the tears stopped. Instead she pressed Barbie to her face and kissed the doll noisily, her eyes locked on her mother. Emma's throat tightened.

"Don't you ever put her down?" She flinched inwardly at the harshness of her own voice. Lily paused, a sudden furrow creasing her soft skin, as she seemed to cast around for the right answer, then shook her head slowly. No, of course you don't, Emma thought.

Since Barbie's arrival on Lily's fourth birthday – an ill-conceived gift from one of Nick's aunts, the doll had become a fixture in family life. Emma had worried about Lily's instant love affair with this confection of blonde and pink, and had tried everything to cajole her daughter back to her rather, well, more educational toys. Nick had found the whole thing funny, told her not to worry, that soon enough "Babs' would grow dull and would be consigned to the deepest recesses of the toy box. He had been right. Barbie had started to look more disheveled, more tattered than high-maintenance, and eventually spent a long winter's week outside in the garden, unnoticed. Both parents had breathed a sigh of relief. But after Nick had gone, and with no apparent explanation, Barbie had re-appeared and from then on was never out of Lily's grasp. Emma had even been forced to buy the doll an entire new wardrobe, each ballgown, cheerleader outfit, sequined leotard guaranteeing a brief window of quiet. Now, wherever she turned it seemed that Barbie was there, her blue eyes staring blankly and, was it her imagination, with a hint of triumph in her big baby blue eyes.

"Mummy?" Lily's whisper broke across her thoughts, "I need a wee."

They walked home in a silence punctuated by the skittering and scraping of Lily's shoes against the tarmac. She glanced at her mother slyly with each scuff, wanting and yet not wanting a response. The streets were quiet, bay windows blank and beautifully clean. Draped with expensive curtains and vases of delicately arranged flowers. Dressed, ready and waiting for the front door to slam and life flood the house once more. Emma could picture the all too familiar life inside. Tasteful decoration, carefully planned bookcases, shabby but beautiful hand-me-down kitchen tables. The shine of success, a coordinated tight-knit of family.

Normally Emma would glance at each window as they passed, but today she kept her eyes fixed on the pavement and quickened her pace. "Come on Lily, we don't have all day".

"Barbie's tired" Lily observed happily, skipping alongside her mother's fast heels. She was hopeful of conversation. Lily had misty memories of long chats with her mother, about all the important things - ducks in the park, why gran was so wrinkly, how she could become a princess, but would in fact rather be a pony. There was no response, today, as with all days, would be a quiet day. Emma looked down at her daughter, the sunlight darting through Lily's impossibly blonde hair. The ever present bloody Barbie, the one and only subject of importance as far as her daughter was concerned.

The doll had even attended the funeral, and as the heavy earth clattered on his coffin, there was Barbie swinging back and forth in Lily's tight grip – her pink ice dancer costume a cruel flash of a different life, where on this particular Wednesday Emma and Lily should have been finger painting, or reading, Lily's chatter warming kitchen, waiting for the return of husband and father. Instead they stood hunched and numb against the drizzle, and buried him. Emma had hated Barbie ever since.

The weeks after the funeral passed, Emma remained strong – tight smiles and dry eyes. Well, she had to, her friends agreed, for Lily's sake, besides, and not wanting to put too fine a point on it, she was still young, she would heal, and on cue, a replacement would be found and life could go on. If anyone had stopped long enough, between coffees, and dropping in with casseroles that would go uneaten, if anyone had stopped to look, rather than avoiding her eyes with regretful smiles, they would have seen, clearly, easily seen, that she was not strong. Just disbelieving.

Young men with wives and five year olds, with friends, holidays booked and plans to watch the football do not die. They do not simply disappear under a mess of tubes and dressings and "we did everything we coulds". They carried on, they came back with a weak smile, a squeezed hand and a croaked joke. But, as Emma learnt, disbelief will only last you so long. Two months long to be precise. Eight weeks to the day dawned and Emma came face to face with belief. Now, nowhere was safe. Every thought, action, inanimate object, was capable of slamming her to the floor, paralyzed with grief. On the fourth day she cried on the kitchen floor for three hours, aware but unthinking as the microwave clock winked away the time. Lily had crawled wide-eyed on to her lap and gently stroked her arms; Emma ignored her. The face was too much.

At other times she would call his mobile, although it had long since been disconnected, hoping to catch him out, her heart beating faster at the just-maybe of each call. Desperate and certain in equal measure. On her own mobile were ten or so texts which she guarded, scrolled through, read and re-read. Inane messages about pints of milk and football practice, scattered with the occasional kiss. Three weeks after belief had set in, she had found Lily in the bathroom, shaking and eyes open wide, confused but consumed with terror. Emma's mobile phone bobbed in the water of the toilet bowl. The texts never returned. A slap tingled, unused, in Emma's hand. She sent Lily to her room and shut the door, then retreated to her own room and sat at the end of the bed. She watched disinterestedly as afternoon turned to dusk, then to a heavy evening gloom. At one point she heard the creak of Lily's door open, a held-breath pause and then the door pulled tight once more.

Three months passed, work wondered where she was and if she was coming back. She didn't know and she wasn't. Her friends, once so admiring of her strength shrank back from the spit and the storm. They retreated to their companionable nights on the sofa, shuddering at the thought how lucky they were, and how it could have been anyone, but thank God it hadn't been them.

They turned the corner onto their street, Emma expecting the now familiar push-me-pull-you of love and hatred as they reached the front gate. Her mother had suggested she sell it, considering how expensive it was and that there was now barely any money coming in. Her mother had paused, gently touched her arm, and asked if she'd thought about selling the house? It was far too big for just the two of them, and she herself had seen some lovely, cheaper flats in town, where they would be perfectly happy. Emma had not spoken to her since.

"Look mummy" Her daughter had collected the post, and held it aloft, a pleased smile spread across her face. Emma flicked through it absentmindedly as Lily stood to attention, waiting eagerly for her "well done'. At the last envelope Emma's stomach dropped, she yanked open the hall sideboard and shoved it in with the other letters, all branded "FINAL NOTICE' in angry red letters. She shut the drawer with a slam and Lily sidled into the lounge. Emma remained in the hall, running her hand along the top of the dark walnut of the sideboard, listening to the chirruping of children's television which suddenly filled the cool quiet of the hall. Lily had long since learnt the art of TV and DVD.

She drifted to the door of the lounge. Her daughter sat transfixed, knees drawn up and huddled in one of Nick's old jumpers. It was ridiculous, Emma knew, to worry about that jumper. Its comfort had long since faded, the smell rubbed away by months of strange skin. Lily had claimed it for herself, but Emma had taken it from her daughters' bed. She felt a hot stab of annoyance. Lily must have crept into her room and taken it back and was set on mauling it, reducing it to little more than a rag.

"Lily, why are you wearing that please? You're spoiling it young lady." Emma's voice cut sharply through the primary colored chatter of the TV. Lily looked up at her, bewildered

"Don't give me that look. I have told you before, more than once. Now take it off."

Emma stepped towards her daughter and held her hand out for the jumper. The material clinging to Lily's knees had already begun to shine with wear. Lily pursed her lips and shook her head.

"Do not push me Lily. I have had a long day. Now I will count to ten and you will take that jumper off." She leant down and moved to yank the jumper over her daughter's head.

"No, no, no, no" Lily shouted, arms flailing, the Barbie doll's hard plastic pushed into her mother's face. Emma wrenched the doll from her daughter's iron grip, the force sending it flying across the room where it slammed into the window with a reverberating clank. The struggle stopped. Lily dropped her arms, her body limp and allowed the jumper to be peeled from her. Lily's hair stuck to her face, purple with the heat of battle. They glared at each other. In the corner of her eye, Emma could see the doll - arms skewed weirdly, eyes staring blankly at the ceiling. Her daughter quietly crawled to the window and carefully picked her doll up, smoothed her hair and turned back to the television. Emma dropped her gaze and concentrated on folding and re-folding the jumper, biting down on the thoughts which clambered and crowded inside.

"Mummy?"

"Yes?" Emma's voice was faint, the warm wool in her hands suddenly scalding her skin. She needed some air.

"Can I have one of those?"

She was pointing at a frenetic advert which was swirling around the screen.

"Of course we can," Emma forced a brightness into her voice, "we'll go shopping tomorrow."

Lily bunched her shoulders in delight and turned to share her familiar smile, but the doorway was already empty.

Shredding the Label

By Helen Hunt

Looking at Cathy always *was* like looking in a mirror. I watch as she strokes her finger across her lips. She leaves a trail like snail slime. It always irritates me when she does that, clagging up the rim of the glass. I'll have to wash that up later....

She's pouring me another glass of wine. As my nose hovers over the top of the glass, I breathe in the alcohol fumes. I just need her to be a little more tipsy than I am. Then I can talk to her....

I wonder where to start. I slosh my wine gently and a thousand rainbows dance around my glass. Why do they call it red wine I wonder, when really it's purple? Like red grapes are really purple and white grapes are really green.

"You know – the thing that happened...."

"Oh Maggie – don't get started on that again, please. I've told you before. It's best not to think about it. We can't just backtrack on all of those years. '

"Why not? She backtracked on the first six years of our lives." My glass shakes and dark droplets slip onto the tablecloth.

"I don't think she did it on purpose." She brushes the drops away with her fingers, staining the ends with boozy stigmata.

"You don't know that do you?"

"Does it really matter?"

"It does to me." I must keep hold of my temper. Especially today.

"But how can we tell her? How can we tell anyone? I don't see why it matters anyway."

"Of course it matters. Don't you care how I've felt all these years?" Now she's sprinkling salt on the blotches of wine on the tablecloth. The salt sucks up the liquid and slowly turns pink. The stain is still there though – underneath.

And I wonder if she knows how much I resent her. She thinks I'm jealous of her – but I'm not. It's a bit more complicated than that.

"Of course I care', she's half way down her second glass of Merlot. "But I didn't feel any different."

"You must have."

"No – we were so close. We shared everything."

"Not quite everything."

"But that was afterwards… a long time after."

I refill her glass. The red wine splashes and gurgles from the bottle. The bottle zings against the glass, but this time I don't spill any.

"But if I'd still been you it wouldn't have happened to me. It would have happened to you." Does that sound selfish I wonder?

"No it wouldn't. That's ridiculous. How can that be true?"

"It is true." It isn't, of course, I just wish it was. It's funny how some people's lives just seem to be programmed to go a certain way….

"Maggie – don't." The wine has stained her lips now; all mixed in with that horrible stuff she slaps on them.

"They always say that the mother can tell the difference even if no one else can. It's meant to be almost a psychic thing. So why did she get it wrong? It shouldn't be possible. She should have known! And if she had known it wouldn't have happened would it?"

"Well according to you, it would. It just would have happened to me instead. I suppose that would be all right?"

And that's the kind of thing that really makes me want to slap her. Why should I pay the price for having my destiny stolen and replaced with a nightmare?

"Did you ever think about asking her?"

"No. I think the problem was that we both just accepted it. We were six… it's just that at that age… well, you think your parents are always right don't you?"

"Maybe if we'd had a father, things would have been different."

"You mean he might have been able to tell us apart?"

"No, I just mean different generally."

Oh yes. A father would have made things different. A father and not just a succession of "uncles', each worse than the last. Well maybe not quite that … one was definitely worse than the others. But I can't even remember where he came in the long procession.

"Sometimes I thought I'd got it wrong… and I just imagined that it happened…."

Well, it's all very well for you to say that isn't it my smug sister? You didn't imagine it. Not any of it.

"More wine?"

She puts her hand over the top of the glass, but I playfully slap it away. I top up my glass as well and hope she won't notice I'm not actually drinking that much of it

"The thing is…', she says… "now I've met Gavin. None of that… stuff… matters any more."

I clench my fists against the chair. How can she say that? How can my sister be so self-satisfied and predictable? Easier for her than for me of course.

When you watch films where people have swapped identities, it's always supposed to be funny, clever or a big adventure. No one ever mentions what it's like when you're the one that, well, loses out. What if I don't want to be Maggie? What if I want to go back to being Cathy. Cathy – the happy one, the well balanced one, the one that's never been any trouble.

I am Cathy. But no one will believe me. After all, how could a mother make a mistake like that? Mothers always know don't they? But what if just a moment's absent-mindedness results in a twist in fortunes that rollercoasters out of control? I get a corkscrew and open another bottle.

"So, how are the wedding plans going, Cathy?" I say. In my head I say Maggie but I won't say that aloud.

"I've got to get my birth certificate from Mum so that Gav can go and get the marriage licence."

You see there's another conundrum. If my birth certificate says I'm Cathy, does that make me Cathy? Or Maggie? It's not like your birth certificate's actually part of you is it? It's not stapled to your head or anything. It's not tattooed on your leg or welded to your DNA. Apparently it happened a lot in the blitz. People would just walk out of a bombed building with someone else's identity. It's like all those Agatha Christie stories where everyone turns out to be someone else....

Of course no one ever believed what I said anyway. I tried to tell people I was Cathy. And everyone just said "Oh, what funny tricks you girls play. Now do be sensible, Maggie." And I tried to tell people about the other thing as well, but I couldn't get the words out. Maggie knows though... we used to share a room....

Even when I was sent to the school counsellor all those times, for being naughty, I didn't say anything. Well, it didn't help when they always started by saying "Of course – you're Cathy's sister." And then they'd look at me as if they couldn't believe that Cathy's sister could be naughty. Well, if only they'd known the truth....

And no one listens to me now. "It's the drink talking', they say. She hasn't noticed how many times I've topped up her glass. It's amazing how easily distracted she is. You just have to mention the wedding.... Gav's nice you know. And I can't help wondering why he wants her and not me... not when we look so alike. I've never had a boyfriend though. You should see the bridesmaid's dress she wants me to wear! I haven't told her yet that I'm not going to wear it... she won't like it when she finds out....

"I'll get another bottle from upstairs, Mags', she says. "That one's nearly dead."

Yes it is. I've waited a long time for this talk, so a break while she goes upstairs is nothing. Not compared to the other breaks. Cathy went to university, then had a gap year. She sent me lots of postcards of India – nice of her really. All those white hot beaches. She might have been trying to rub it in… but I gave her the benefit of the doubt.

I pour the dregs of the last bottle into her glass. Little bits of red residue from the bottom of the bottle mix in with the wine already in there and slowly float to the bottom. I walk over to the sink and tip the rest of my glass away. I run the taps to get rid of the smell of the alcohol. If only everything could be swilled away that easily.…

"Valpolicella?"

"Yes, fine', I say. I don't care – I'm not going to drink it!

She pours it like a waitress. Or a barmaid. Like everything she does, it is professional and crisp. She isn't drunk enough yet. She tucks her hair behind her ears, hair that's brown like chocolate, Gav says – apparently. They make a lovely couple. He's just the right height to make her look petite and fragile. And his white chocolate hair makes him look much younger than he is.

I sip the Valpolicella. Not as good as the Merlot. But maybe she won't notice. And maybe she won't notice the ground up powder mixed with the sediment in her glass. That should just give her a bit of a nudge in the right direction.

"Don't you think Gavin ought to know about all this?" I ask, as I run my finger around the top of my glass, dipping it first in the wine so that it squeaks and resonates. "No secrets when you're in love are there?" Not that I'd know. Not that I've ever had the chance to find out. Not about real love anyway – just that other thing. That thing that wasn't love; and that was forced on me when I was too young to say no.…

I pick half the label off the wine bottle and shred it with my fingers. I'm not bitter. What is it they say? Don't get mad, get even! OK then.

"Another glass of wine?" I say, and she holds her hand out to me. The diamond twinkles and refracts light across the table. Globes of light settle on the piles of pink salt and illuminate them.

"Thanks, Sis." I wish she wouldn't say that.

I tip the bottle so that wine pours freely into her glass. Right to the top so she can hardly lift it.

"Sip a bit first," I say. She slurps and we both laugh.

"Thanks… Sis', she says, again.

"You know I love you Mags. I'm sorry about all the other stuff. Sorry, y'know?" she says. As her voice begins to slur, I wait patiently for my moment to come.

"Have another glass, Maggie," I say. I hold my breath….

"Yeah. …' she says, "thanks."

My heart stops beating. I don't want to push my luck, so I slosh more wine into her glass and sit back in my chair. I resist the temptation to bite my nails. Cathy doesn't bite her nails. They'll need to be beautifully manicured for the wedding…. Cathy's growing her hair for the wedding as well. I unclip mine from the top of my head and let it fall on to my shoulders.

When we were really little – and I was Cathy – we laughed all the time. At the park, on the swings, going round and round on the roundabout – our pigtails touching the floor in a daredevil dance. I loved Maggie then. We didn't need anyone else – not even our mother. Maybe she resented that. Then for some reason, I was Maggie. I knew I was Maggie because Mummy called me Maggie – so I had to be. It's not the kind of thing you argue with. And it's not like anyone else could tell us apart. And then – it didn't really matter. Maggie and Cathy. Cathy and Maggie. Interchangeable – almost.

Even then – it would have been OK. If the other thing hadn't happened. Or if it hadn't happened to me. I gasp a mouthful of wine down to stop the angry tears from coming. She is slumped across the table now. Three bottles down – yes that should do it. I look at her face. My face. She sighs slightly through the alcoholic fug. Slowly, so slowly and gently, I ease the ring off her finger and on to mine. I pick up her mobile phone from the table where she has put it down.

"Mum, it's Cathy. I'm just coming over to get my birth certificate for the marriage thing. Maggie? Oh yes, Maggie's fine. I'm going to take her home first. She's had a bit too much to drink again… but I'm sure she'll be all right."

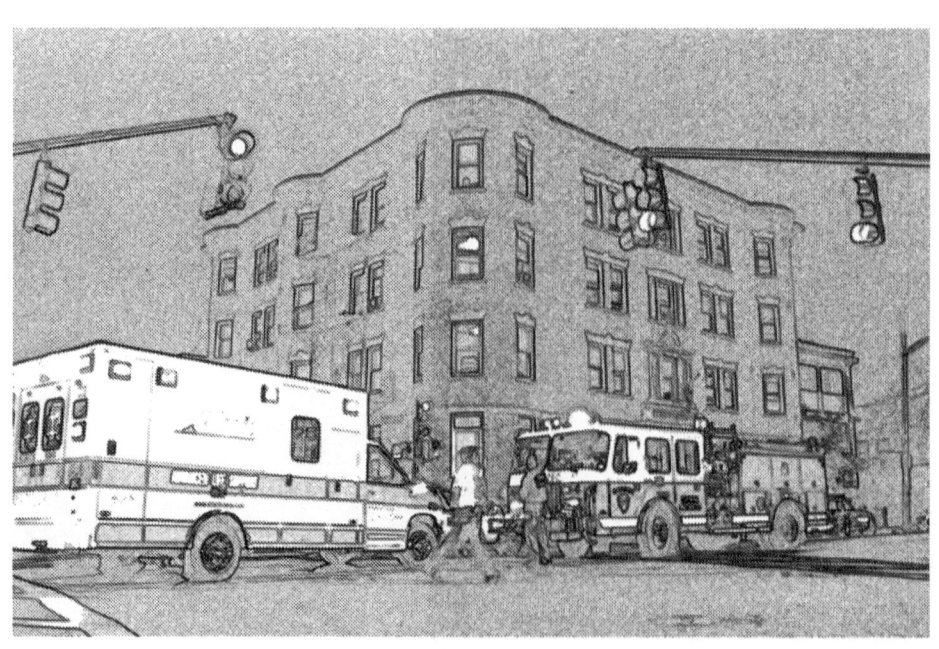

Ash

(Honorable Mention)

By Virginia Baily

In the olden days, when stuff mattered, Rose used to do all kinds of things. She used to hang out in the park and watch boys screeching about on their skateboards and pretend not to be impressed. She used to chat online to her friends and swap music. She used to go to Bethany's house and work out complicated dance routines. She used to read. She sat on her bed by the window, wriggling her toes inside the giant shoe and looking at the shelves full of books above her desk. She used to read masses, with Billy sitting on her lap. He was pawing at the door right now as if he missed the olden days too.

The giant shoe didn't belong to the olden days. It came from just now. It was red like blood and wine and forbidden things. And if you sniffed it you caught an animal smell, a gasp of wildness from a dark forest. Rose's foot looked sad and pathetic inside it, like a little animal waiting to be born. She hooked it off and stroked the soft leather, remembering the dance. How she had been propelled around her bedroom, her toes curling to grip his long bony ones, his feet her shifting floor. Not dancing so much as being danced. Magic.

She slid off the bed and opened the door to let Billy in. He rushed at her legs and rubbed against her, purring and pressing as he circled. Rose pushed him away with her foot and held him off as she swung the shoe in a wide arc and cast a spell. She imagined an army of faithful retainers springing into life, ready to do her bidding.

"Go forth and seek the owner of this red shoe," she commanded them. "Ensure that no young man is forgotten. He whom the shoe fits, bring him to me. Or text me on my mobile and I will direct my trusty steed to carry me thither."

Her trusty steed, or bicycle, had already carried her everywhere she could think of on this quest. She had peered into cafes and bars, toured the parks, cycled the suburbs. All of Anne-Marie's other friends put in regular appearances, but not the boy with the red shoes. He had vanished. She dropped the shoe to the floor and kicked it under the bed. Billy pressed himself urgently against her again, thwacking her ankles with his tail. She bent to pick him up.

"What's the matter with *you*?" she said as he clawed to break free. He ran to the door and she followed. She paused half way down the stairs to listen. What was it? She could hear the clock in the kitchen ticking and the fridge humming. Further away, outside the house, there was a faint buzz of traffic, but nothing else. She was listening to emptiness. No voices in the house. No radio or TV or chatting or music or anything. The cat, who'd run ahead into the kitchen, bounded back into the hallway and looked up at her. He meowed his most pitiful meow and she put her hand on the banister, sticky against her fingers, and went on down. The door to the dining room was ajar and she pulled it to without looking in.

In the kitchen, breakfast leftovers still littered the table. A bowl with bits of muesli stuck to the sides at her father's place, toast crumbs on a plate with a little smear of butter where Rose herself had sat. "I'll wash up Dad," she'd said. An unopened tin of cat food stood on the side. "I'll feed Billy," she'd said. "Go on, Mum's waiting for you."

The clock above the sink said quarter to one. One or other of her parents would be back soon. She had to feed Billy, load the dishwasher and wipe the table. That was all. The tin-opener wouldn't work. It wouldn't pierce the top of the can. She found an old box of cat biscuits at the back of the cupboard with a few left in the bottom and tipped them into Billy's bowl. They were mostly dust. It wasn't what he wanted, she could see. She swept crumbs off plates and into the bin with her fingers like her Mother did and stacked the dishes in the machine. She couldn't tell if there were enough dishes in there to justify switching it on. She crouched next to Billy, who was sniffing the biscuit dust suspiciously and stroked the back of his head. "It doesn't matter," she said.

She put the kettle on, thinking she would make herself a cup of tea but instead she went back up to her room and fetched the shoe out from under the bed. "Come on," she said. "Show me." She leant against the headboard, and closed her eyes, trying to make a wish. She didn't believe in fairy tales. It wasn't that. But she sort of believed in signs and omens because there had to be reasons for stuff happening. She clutched the shoe for comfort, rocking to and fro at the memory of the police at the door that night, Anne-Marie's 18th birthday party.

It had taken a lot of emotional blackmail on her big sister's part, as well as getting two As and a B for her A-levels, to persuade their parents to stay away the night. Rose's sleepover was mysteriously cancelled and it was too late to make other arrangements. Anne-Marie had thrown a wobbly. She was supposed to be celebrating not bloody babysitting, she said, so Rose had promised to stay in her room and watch a DVD.

Once their parents had gone, Rose ran upstairs and pulled on the white backless dress she'd bought on holiday, tucked a pink rose behind her ear and splashed some perfume around her throat, certain Anne-Marie would relent, but no way. "It's my night Rosie," she said. Rose cut another deal – glass of champagne on the hour or she'd come downstairs and behave embarrassingly.

She turned off the lights in her room, lit candles and incense, daubed her mouth a pearly pink and sat sulkily on the window ledge. The music strained at the canvas of the marquee in the garden, people shrieked with laughter and the laser lights bounced into the night. When her third drink was 10 minutes overdue, she started pacing the room, occasionally stamping and kicking the skirting boards with her pointy silver shoes.

She heard giggling and whispering outside on the landing but no one came. She inched the door open. A tremulous flutter ran through her as if she were on the brink of an adventure. The bathroom clicked open and a young man emerged. He passed so close that Rose could smell him, a familiar resinous scent she could not name but which whooshed up her nostrils. She clung to the cool brass of the doorknob. If she let go she would melt like butter in the sun and so she hung on, printing the serrated pattern into her palm as she printed the boy into her consciousness. She took in the shimmer of his loose red shirt, the way his long legs glided in the black leather trousers and how his black hair was seized back into a thick ponytail. His feet were bare. The memory now, as she held one of his shoes in her hands, caused her stomach to cramp.

At the turn in the stairs he glanced back and he seemed to wink before disappearing beyond her field of vision. The bathroom jolted open again and a bedraggled girl tottered out, muttering. Rose knew her vaguely, a college friend of Anne-Marie's. Kate. Her hair was dripping as if she'd dunked her head under the tap. Seconds later Anne-Marie herself came out. Must have been crowded in that bathroom.

"What are you doing?" Rose said. Anne-Marie had done something weird to her eyes. They were like muddy puddles. She put her arms around Rose and rested her head heavily on Rose's shoulder. "Where's my champagne?" Her sister gave her a squeeze and pulled away, sniffing as if she were about to sneeze. She spoke like an actress in a dubbed film, making unnecessary shapes with her mouth. Her tongue was getting in the way.

"Shend tup pronto," she said.

"What?"

"Na minute."

Anne Marie flapped her hand indecipherably and made her way downstairs, gripping the banister with one hand and walking her fingers down the wall with the other.

It was the boy in red who came. He had a bag slung over his shoulder and a tray with two glasses and a bottle of champagne balanced on the palm of one hand. He bowed low, folding himself down from his great height and held himself there while Rose wondered what to say. Her heart thudded against her ribcage. She noticed the asymmetrical design of his shirt, with black dots covering one sleeve and thought of ladybirds, wondering if all ladybirds were ladies and realising that they couldn't be, of course. She touched him lightly on the shoulder and, as if she'd broken the spell on him, he unfurled.

"Milady Rose, than whom no flower is more sweetly petalled nor more lovely in its budding bloom, your humble servant is sent by Princess Anne-Marie to offer you refreshment," he said and then he laughed. Rose put her hand over her mouth so he wouldn't see her brace.

"May I?" he asked, indicating the floor with a sweep of his hand. She nodded permission and he sat cross-legged to pop the cork. They were the best glasses from the cabinet in the dining room. She tipped the drink too quickly down her throat so the bubbles frothed in her nose and made her snort.

"What's in your bag?" she asked, to cover her embarrassment.

"Money, smokes, gear," he said. She didn't know what gear might be but she nodded.

"You don't look like your sister," he said. This was true. Where Anne Marie was soft and rounded with brown wavy hair and freckles, Rose was tall and skinny and her hair hung straight in a gingery gold plait. She knew she'd changed over the last year, but this boy was looking at her as if she were an exotic flavor of ice-cream. Butterscotch perhaps.

"*Are* you like her though?"

"In what way?"

"You know," he said, raising one eyebrow. But she didn't. He filled their glasses again and stood up. "Dance?" he asked, holding out his free hand.

"Don't you want to get back to the party?"

"This is the party Rose. Right here."

He drained his glass, pulled her to her feet and held her own glass to her lips, feeding her like a fledgling until it was empty. Her face was level with the hollow at the base of his throat. She turned her head sideways, laying her cheek against his chest.

The banging at the front door began when they were swirling in slow circles around the dusky cloud of her floating bedroom. A clattering, violent shock of insistent knocks, accompanied by loud, authoritative voices. His hands on her back tightened and she felt his heart echo the bang and pulse suddenly against her cheek.

"What's that?" she whispered.

"Can you do me a favour?" he asked, gazing blankly over her head. "Get my shoes for me. They're by the front door." She waited. "Now," he said, dropping his eyes to hers. Black eyes.

She slid down the stairs, ignoring the uniformed men crowding into the kitchen, the shouts and sound of crying. She barely glanced at the jumble of trainers because she'd already spotted the ones that had to be his. She plucked the red shoes from beside the mat, fast as a cat, and was back in her room in the space of a breath. He was waiting by the window.

"It's the police," she said. He didn't speak as he took the shoes from her, tied the laces together and draped them round his neck.

"What are you doing?"

"We don't get on, me and the police," he said, swinging one leg out. He bent towards her and brushed her mouth with his, champagne lips fizzing, before dropping out onto the kitchen roof.

It was a homemade marquee. Their father had fixed a plank between the kitchen extension and the apple tree. He'd stretched white canvas across and attached it to wooden struts nailed to the fence so the dining-room no longer opened onto the everyday garden but into a golden billow of a ballroom where grape-shaped lanterns hung in twinkling bunches.

"I don't know your name."

"Ash," he said as he shifted his weight onto the plank. Unhurried, as if oblivious to the blare of the ambulance siren now shivering through the abrupt silence – someone had pulled the plug on the music - he stepped forward. His feet were turned out like a tightrope walker, big toes bent upwards from the strain. She'd held her breath and crossed her fingers to keep him from falling as he swayed in the middle where the plank was springiest. He'd lurched sideways, flapped his hands like wings and righted himself. As he reached out and pulled into the safety of the apple tree, its foliage enclosing him, Rose's bedside clock had flashed midnight and a policeman burst into her room.

She hadn't seen Ash drop from the tree. It was as if he'd stepped into another world.

She'd found the shoe the next morning lying underneath her old swing, like a giant ladybird crouching in the muddy patch where her feet had scuffed the grass away. She'd known what it meant straightaway. It was a clue. She didn't show it to her parents. They were taking it in turns at the hospital, sitting by Anne-Marie's bed. They wanted to be there when she woke up, if she woke up. She would wake up. Kate had woken up after three days, but it was nearly a week.

Rose got off the bed and peered out her window. The marquee flapped forgotten and forlorn below. She examined the wobbly plank that led to the place Ash had gone, imagining how and where she would have to place her feet.

When she went downstairs to make a cup of tea, she put the sharp knife in her pocket and collected Billy to keep her company. She climbed onto the window ledge and waited for midnight.

The Evangelist

By Mel Fawcett

Less than two years ago this summer two things happened on a single day that combined to change my life. Firstly, as I was commuting to work in the city – (unbelievable though it now seems, I had been making that same journey one way or another for nearly thirty years) – I was sitting on the underground train when a tall, middle-aged black man entered the carriage and started preaching the word of God. Hardly anyone looked his way. Most people were either reading – and most of them the free morning newspaper - or listening to music through earphones and staring straight ahead, while still others were sitting there with their eyes closed. I think I was the only one openly looking at the black man. Over his suit, he was wearing a placard which proclaimed that Jesus had died for our sins. He was telling everyone that they should be reading the bible and harkening to the word of God. Although he had a strong voice, his words did sometimes get lost in the noise of the train. I felt slightly embarrassed for him because no one appeared to be paying any attention. After a few minutes, I got tired of his message myself and returned to my book. When I next looked up, he had gone.

The second thing that happened was on the way home. This time I was standing on a crowded platform with a lot of other commuters, waiting for the next train. A burly youth of no more than seventeen or eighteen was pushing his way along the platform when someone swore at him. The youth stopped and turned abruptly to the man who swore. An argument started and quickly, stupidly escalated into threats of violence. Then, unbelievably, the youth pulled out a knife and without another word, stuck it into the belly of the other man. A woman screamed.

The victim slumped onto the platform as the train came in. Everyone standing nearby was retreating. As soon as the doors opened, we all hurried onto the train. I didn't see what happened to the youth with the knife, but at least two passengers standing near the doors got their mobile phones out and photographed the victim writhing on the platform. Meanwhile, people on the platform were walking round and stepping over him. No one went to his aid. Maybe they thought he was drunk, or maybe they were afraid of getting involved. I regretted having got on the train, but it was too late to get off again. The doors had closed and I was too self-conscious to pull the emergency handle. There I felt a huge sigh of relief as the train moved away.

I think I was more upset about my reaction to the stabbing than to the stabbing itself. I couldn't believe how selfish and heartless we had all been. How could we have all acted so callously? The guilt and the anger kept me up most of that night.

I didn't go to work the next day. It wasn't simply that I was tired after a bad night's sleep, and certainly not because I was frightened of knife-wielding youths; it was more because I was so horrified by the violence and by everyone's reaction to it that sitting in an office juggling figures seemed totally irrelevant and meaningless.

During the days that followed, I thought about it a lot, to such an extent that I knew I had to do something. By the time the weekend came, I knew what it was. I was having breakfast with my wife, Jane, and I told her I had decided to take early retirement. Although she was surprised, she didn't object – we were comfortably off and she had a very well-paid job which she enjoyed - but she seemed concerned that I might get bored.

"There's no chance of that," I said. "There's too much to do."

"Like what?" she said with a quizzical smile.

"Like encouraging people to care about one another."

"Come again?"

I'd already told her about the stabbing and the black man and now I told her again.

"Are you telling me you're going to become some kind of evangelist?"

"If that's what you call someone who spreads love and peace, yes."

"Love and peace? Didn't that die out with flower power in the sixties?"

"Maybe. Maybe that's why it needs bringing back."

Jane didn't think I'd go through with it. Even when I told her I'd given my notice in at work she thought I'd change my mind before the notice was up. She didn't seem to understand how important this was to me. Not that I was over eager to get out there and do it; on the contrary – I was terrified of the thought. The prospect of addressing a carriage full of strangers filled me with dread.

When it came to it, I thought I was going to be sick. I'll never forget that first morning. The underground train was crowded and I was standing by the door. I hadn't rehearsed what to say. I wanted to keep it natural; so I just blurted out the first thing that came into my head.

"All change!" I cried. "All change!"

Most passengers looked at me and then at one another.

"That's right, everyone has to change."

Some of them stood up.

"It's all right, there's no need to get up. I don't mean change trains. I mean we have to change out lives. We all need to change the way we live."

A few people smiled when they realized what was going on, but they were in the minority. Most people looked annoyed. I apologized for worrying them and I told them why I was addressing them. I told them about the stabbing, about how everyone had reacted, about the selfishness, about how ashamed I was.

"I was so sickened by my own behavior that I had to do something about it, which is why I'm here today. We should be looking out for each other, not turning our backs or taking bloody photographs to laugh about afterwards. I don't care whether you're Christian, Muslim, Jewish or Hindu, we're all in this life together, we're all human beings – so shouldn't we be helping one another?"

I talked for about half an hour. People got on and off and some sat through my whole spiel. I surprised myself how long I went on for. But it really took it out of me. When I got off the train, I was shaking and on the point of collapse.

Even so, I did it every day after that. And once I got into my stride, I was doing it during every rush hour, morning and evening, and often during the day as well. Although I never liked starting and although I invariably felt shattered by the time I'd finished, while I was doing it I felt all right. Of course most people ignored me and occasionally someone even told me to shut up. But then there were the ones who nodded in agreement with what I said, and one or two people even came up to me and said it was decent and courageous thing I was doing and that made me feel good.

The worst part was the rare occasions when I was physically abused. The first time it happened was when an aggressive young man elbowed me in the face. He pretended it was an accident but there was too much build-up for it to be accidental. He'd been looking daggers at me ever since I started addressing the carriage of early-morning commuters. If I'd had any sense I would have seen the signs and quit before it was too late. I remember being relieved when I saw him getting up, but on his way out he caught me with a vicious jerk of his elbow right on the bridge of my nose. And then he had the nerve to apologize. I was in too much pain to say anything. I staggered onto the platform and collapsed onto a bench. I thought my nose was broken, it swelled up so quickly. I had to sit there for ages. Eventually, I felt steady enough to stand up and go home. When Jane saw me that evening she screamed. I did look a dreadful sight, with two black eyes and a swollen nose. She said she hoped I had learnt my lesson. She assumed I was going to stop. But, although I was in considerable discomfort, I disagreed with her about stopping. In fact, as far as I was concerned, it was all the more reason to carry on. If people were violent against someone who was only trying to get them to care about one another, then there was a definite need for my message.

So the following day, with two very dark eyes and a still-swollen nose - I got on a train and explained to the passengers that I looked the way I did because I'd been hit in the face. I told them how it gave me more reason than ever to carry on. I even made a joke that if anyone felt like beating me up it

The third time I was attacked was undoubtedly the worst- both in physical hurt and viciousness of intent. Three kids - I guess they were about fourteen - followed me off the train and jumped me in a deserted underpass. They laid into me with fists and boots. I shouted for them to stop and I tried to protect myself, but I didn't fight back; I thought that would be hypocritical. I don't think the attack had anything to do with my message; I think with them it was just mindless violence. That really saddened me. I can't remember how I got home, but I do remember that Jane refused to acknowledge my injuries. She wouldn't talk to me. She didn't talk to me for days.

Don't get me wrong about the violence. It didn't happen that often, and it was only very rare that I was hurt. Most days were without incident. Some days were very rewarding. I even had a couple of American kids who wanted to be my followers. They were very sincere and I think they were hurt when told them I wasn't looking for followers; I was simply spreading a message. But afterwards, I sort of regretted turning them away and it made me wonder whether I should be involving other people. I would have like to have discussed it with Jane, but when she did finally start talking to me again it was to tell me that if I didn't stop what I was doing she was going to leave me. That shook me more than the violence.

"But you can't. We're married."

"Are we? I'm not so sure. I married a sensible and responsible man. You are no longer the man I married."

I told her I was sorry that she didn't like what I was doing and that I would be devastated if she ever left me.

"But please don't ask me to give up my life's work."

"It's not your life's work; you've only been doing it for eight or nine months."

"But it's what I was meant to do and it's what I will be doing for the rest of my life. Can't you can understand that?"

"No, I can't. Why can't you understand that I don't want to get a call from some hospital to say you've been beaten half to death."

I would have done anything to stop her leaving me, anything except giving up what I was doing. I couldn't do that, even for her. So that's what happened in the end. Jane left me. And for the past twelve months I've been coming home to an empty house and I hate it.

On the positive side, being alone makes me stay out more and spread my message of hope. As much as I miss Jane, I still think I'm right to be doing what I'm doing. Everyone has to do what they can. I wish she would understand that. We're still in touch and I'm hopeful that one day she'll come back to me. I'm also hopeful that one day people will care more about one another. Maybe I'll be proven right on both counts.

Renovation
Third Prize

By Victoria Adams

The mirror was smeared and cracked in one corner. Bars like these, she thinks, bars like these are run by men. They never come in here, so they don't care how it looks. They don't think how nice it would be with a lick of paint, or if the toilet seat was fixed. The girl next to her is checking out Alexia's new handbag. Damn right she should. Cost fifty quid. Had to pretend she was buying it for someone else to justify it. Justify the expense, justify appreciating it, in public, like that. Alexia tries to concentrate on reapplying her lipstick, tries not to watch the other girls watching her. She likes it, likes all the looks. They feel like little fingers all over her body, running through her hair, stroking her flat stomach. Can they tell I have a six-pack, she wonders. Do they see how slender my hips are. Are they jealous? She has nicer breasts than me, but my legs are longer.

When she presses her lips together to smooth the colour evenly, she shuts her eyes too. And opens them again. A little mental photograph of herself, herself through their eyes. Seeing what they see. She wants to smell what they smell. So, finally, time to go back into the main room. The Ladies is a little sanctuary for Alexia. A girl's place, a space for the femme and the lovely. Out here, with all the pool and the beer and the inappropriate noise levels, is the man's area. It smells worse than the toilets. She wishes they could all meet up someplace else, but there isn't really anywhere appropriate, not in this town. Back at their table, everyone is getting pretty drunk. Alexia prefers to remain simply pretty. She is drinking orange juice, slowly, through a straw. Did I check if I got lipstick on my teeth she wonders. I always forget to do that.

Concentrating on running her tongue around her front teeth, trying to clean them just in case, she misses the start of the fight. One of the girls at the bar is starting on one of her friends. The men make a circle, whoop and jeer. Animals, they're all animals. She includes the men with the girls in her judgement call. It's hard to tell, what with all the yelling, but the fight seems to be about one of their boyfriends. The girls start pushing each other, and that's when the wig falls off. Like a camera coming suddenly into focus, the girl with no hair is suddenly a man. A man in heels and make-up. Oh my god, thinks Alexia. He's screwed now.

Then the whole atmosphere turns nasty. The shouting becomes cruel, and the girl leaves the men to it. Everyone casts the first blow at the same time. Alexia decides to call it a night, before the police arrive. After all, she is only seventeen, it's time for bed. Her last glimpse of the victim is a pale face under a fence of fists, blood smeared like tears all over his face.

She leaves well alone. She leaves the bar alone. Her legs tremble, making her wobble on her heels. Something makes her start to run down the dark street, trying to put as much distance between herself and the fight as possible. After turning a few corners, she has to stop to catch her breath. The kerb-crawlers are out in force, and she can't stay still for long because they've clocked her now. Even moving, head held high, face turned away from the street, doesn't deter them. They want something from her. They've noticed her long legs and her slender hips.

One guy rolls his window down. She ignores him. She tries not to listen to what he's saying, just keeps walking. Then he makes a grab for her, and she has to run again. Not too far from home now. Next time, she promises herself, next time I'll get a cab. But she knows she can't do that, not really. It's a small town and people talk. Her parents don't know she's out. It's a school night. There are so many reasons. Next time I'll wear sensible shoes. Next time won't happen. I won't let this happen again. Next time I'll just stay in.

Her foot turns inside the high heels, and something snaps. Sitting in the gutter, the tears smear her make-up down her cheeks. Then it starts to rain.

Bloody hell, just what I need. Stupid bloody heels. It could be worse; the heel snapped, not her ankle. Still have to walk home in broken bloody shoes though. The rain starts soaking through her clothes, and suddenly everything just gets to her: the fact that it is dark and cold and getting late and quite frankly everyone has been bloody horrible this evening. So much for the fun night out. So much for the new bag and the effort of getting made-up and her hair and so much effort. So tired now. So tired.

Walking unevenly past a plate glass window, she turns her face to avoid the kerb crawlers, and catches herself staring at a ghost. The man from the bar looks back at her, reflected in the window pane. The blood sickens her. All down his face. Then the car passes by and the reflection dims and she realises it's just her, and it's mascara and eyeliner and not blood. So glad it wasn't her. So glad it wasn't her blood. So glad she wasn't in his shoes, his wig, his badly fitting cheap dress. I'm too young for this. For all this crap. I can't wait to leave this small no-town with all those small-minded thugs. Ugly thoughts. Ugly people. Pointless lives.

Then it's her gate. The thick black metal latch clicks down behind her, securing the outside world on the other side of the fence. Just a quiet click, muffled by the rain. And both shoes are off, carried in one hand as she creeps down the side of the path that doesn't set off the security light. Familiar stones, slippery under dirty, wet stocking feet. And the back door isn't double locked; thank god, nobody came down to check. And it lets her slip in then slam click the handle chunk chunk the lock rattle across the chain, and pause in the still, dry dark in case someone heard. The house breathes, hums. The heating is on. No music, no television. It's going to be ok. She won't be caught this time. Back safe, back in the safe and comfort, the adrenaline rush of what she's done comes back. Next time. Next time. Maybe next time she will get a taxi, to the top of the street. Share it with one of the other girls, keep the costs down.

Out of the kitchen now and slowly up the stairs. Tip-toe is crap, flat feet, slowly massaging the carpet, much quieter. Less likely to stumble. Glad she didn't drink. That stair creaks. There's a pile of books on the left here. Then into the room, shut that door. Pull the bolt across. Feel safe again. Open the window, put some music on quiet like. Her hand is shaking as she lights up a final cigarette. Then the action calms her and she can enjoy being still. Enjoy the last bit of the night. Looking at her hands in the dim night light, listening to the quiet rain and the quiet music. So beautiful. Got to remember to take that polish off before I go to school tomorrow.

Or I'll get a row. Don't want to risk that.

One light on, in the corner of the room. Alexia closes the window and the curtain, stands in front of the mirror, and starts to strip. The top lands by a pair of football boots. Her padded bra drapes over a guitar. The skirt was really expensive, so she folds it over a chair, next to a pile of ironing. Shameful slender hips, peel the ruined stockings off and everything else. Let it all hang out. Shameful slender hips. Legs not quite right without the skirt. Oh, though, she misses the bra most. Cupping the flat, flat chest she pretends the breasts, half closes her eyes and visualises them. It doesn't work. One day, she promises herself. One day I'll be really beautiful.

There isn't anything beautiful about the school uniform her mother has laid out for the next day. The grey fabric is rough and coarse, it makes her feel common when she wears it. It doesn't let her say anything about herself. Just as well, she thinks. Just as well. She knocks it off the chair and onto the floor, lets it crumple, pretends to herself it was almost an accident. But now she's too tired to delay this anymore. She has to get to bed. She needs to sleep. The magazines call it beauty sleep. She can't use a phrase like that. She isn't allowed to know about that kind of thing. That kind of thing doesn't go on in a place like this.

The bottom drawer, the locked one, is where she keeps her make-up. And her make-up remover. Slowly it comes off, wiping the layers away. Wiping the mascara from her cheeks.

Don't think about him again. Don't think about that guy in the pub. It couldn't be you. You wouldn't have got involved in the fight in the first place. It won't happen to you. Get a taxi next time though. If there is a next time. Better not to shave tomorrow morning. Just in case. The clothes go in the bottom drawer too. With the broken shoe and the good shoe. And the bag, the lovely beautiful desirable bag. And the wig. And the cotton wool that took the make-up off. And the cigarettes just in case mum comes in to empty the bin. Almost forgot the nails, clean them now. Remove every last trace. Can't avoid it, can't avoid it, can't avoid it. So he looks into the mirror and tries not to recognise his face when it looks back at him. There can't be a next time. This town is too small. It's happening too much, too fast. He can't cry now, not now that Alexia has gone into the drawer. Boys don't cry.

When Alex has left for school the next morning, his mum comes into his room to empty the bin and get his washing. He's forgotten his boots again, she notices. How's he meant to get on at practice without his boots. When she smells the perfume on his shirt she looks for lipstick and, yes, there's a smudge. He's only seventeen she thinks. He's only seventeen. Better not get the girl pregnant. I'll get his father to have a word tonight. What would the neighbours think.

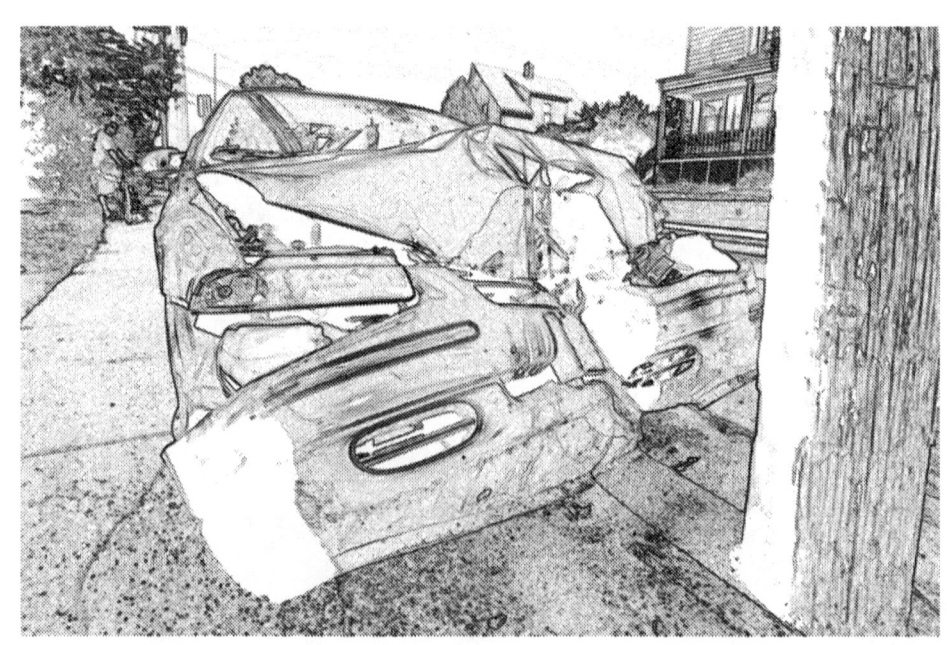

The Photographer
Second Prize

By Kendare Blake

"Show me some of your work."

He glanced down. Now that he was sobering up, he could see that she was not beautiful; her eyes were a little too large and slightly asymmetrical, dark grey in the dim light though he recalled that in the bar they had been blue. He frowned. At least she was still blonde, though even that wasn't quite as he remembered. He had thought that her hair was gold, but now he could see that there were many streaks of brown, and that it was dark at the roots.

"Take your pick," he said, gesturing to the walls with a sweeping motion as he ashed his cigarette into the tray on his bedside table. His walls were filled with framed and matted prints from his previous exhibition, all shades of black and white and grey, peoples' lives in slices, like portions of pizza.

The blonde smiled at him, and lifted her fingers for a drag of his cigarette. He passed it to her, and then watched as she inhaled and passed it back, wrapped herself in a blanket and slipped off of the bed. He reached out to the wall behind him, to bring up the lighting that was strategically placed to enhance the art. A soft, white glow crept along the corners and walls of the gray room. The area around the bed stayed dark. He frowned at the smoke that the blonde exhaled, hanging in the center.

He watched her silently as she walked from photograph to photograph. He was fairly certain that her eyes were unseeing, that her brain was only making feeble clicks and whirrs behind her gray eyes, but he was still curious about what she would say. She had stopped at one of his favorites, a quiet rendering of a man drinking a cup of coffee and reading the newspaper. The headlines screamed across the page before him but his face betrayed no emotion. His eyes, if you looked closely enough, appeared unfocused.

The blonde was leaning forward, her brows puckered like an old woman's mouth. She had done the same thing standing in front of every other piece on the wall. After another moment or two, she turned to him slightly and smiled.

"They're kind of boring," she said apologetically.

He exhaled sharply as he smirked, and crushed out his cigarette. "Really? Is that why the exhibition sold out last year?"

The blonde turned back to the photograph, looking for what she"d missed. She stared helplessly from one shot to the next.

"But, they're just people," she said, confused. "Doing boring things." She walked a few steps to her left. "What is this woman doing? Paying bills?"

He smiled to himself. The photo of the woman paying bills had sold for ten thousand dollars. The reviews for the entire collection had been glowing. He was a collector of human existence, they said. He could take the most mundane aspects of a person's life, and make them sublime. Paying bills, having a headache, cleaning windows; all of the world's boring trivialities were beautiful through his lens. He made his living in the moments that people threw away.

"It really sold out?"

He sighed. "Take that blanket off," he said lazily.

"Why?"

"Because I'm having a hard time remembering why I started talking to you." He watched the struggle on her features. She couldn't decide whether she wanted to be insulted that he had implied she was stupid, or flattered because he had implied he liked her tits.

In the end, she didn't do much of anything, just shrugged again and said, "I guess I was never much for photography. I'm a writer."

He raised his eyebrows at that. "Photos capture images in a way that words can't," he said simply.

"I don't think so," she said, staring at another of his shots, an old woman sleeping in front of the TV. "Photos don't exactly give the viewer very many options, do they? It's just… there. No imagination."

He lit another cigarette. Imagination was frivolous. "I don't need my viewers to create my art for me," he said.

"But there's not much art to it, is there?" She was returning to the bed and gathering up her clothes. "I mean, don't get me wrong, I like photography. I think it's beautiful. But I've always wondered…as an art form, it's so situational. I mean, put me in the middle of Lebanon right now and I could be a photojournalist." She looked back at his walls. "Or that one. The boys waiting for the bus. Put me there, and I could have taken that same picture."

No, you couldn't have, he thought, but said, "When I have a camera, the world holds still for me."

The blonde shrugged dismissively. "When I have a blank page, the world does what I want."

It was time for her to go.

"Would you like to see what I'm working on now?" he asked.

"Of course," she said, and he reached under the bed for his proofs, kept in a rough portfolio binder that catalogued negatives and different developments. He dropped them on the bed in front of her, and then got up and made himself a drink.

He sipped with his back to her, listening to the sounds of the photographs as she leafed through them. He pictured the confusion on her face as she studied each one.

"Well?"

"Um," she said hesitantly, and he turned back.

"My agent says it's a goldmine. The exhibition's in six months. He's talking to a publisher about putting together a coffee table book."

"Who would want these on their coffee table?" She was looking at them with her eyes squinted, her face a mask of varying degrees of shock and disgust.

He ignored her. "I think I'm going to call the collection, "Ugliness"."

"Why would you take pictures of ugly people?" She was looking up at him, a photo in each hand, limp on her lap. He gazed down at them fondly while he drank. One shot was of a woman burned beyond recognition, her face a skeletal scar from which only one bright eye stared out. The other was of a man, screaming into the face of his daughter, his mouth contorted, with spittle flying from his lips.

"Because it's indiscriminate," he said.

"How is ugliness indiscriminate?"

He set his drink down on the nightstand. "Everyone is ugly. All humans are ugly, given enough time."

"But, they're not always."

He waved his hand dismissively. "That's not the story I'm telling," he said, looking carefully at the shot of the girl, sad, with greasy hair and glasses. "It's not done, of course. I'll take a hundred more shots at least." He traced his finger along the face the boy examining the dead dog with a stick. "You couldn't write this, could you," he said smugly.

"I wouldn't want to," she said, and he shrugged, carefully replacing the proofs inside of the portfolio case.

"Well, it's late," he said, placing the case beneath the bed, and reaching for his Nikkon instead. "35 mm," he said as he removed the lens cap. "Everything manual. Gives me more control." He raised the camera to his eye, focusing with a deft movement of fingers and clicked, advanced the film.

"What are you doing?"

"It's for the collection," he said, still taking shots. "I'm going to call it, "slut I met at happy hour."" He continued to work as she pulled on her clothes, her face freezing perfectly in expressions of rage and disgust, her mouth spraying expletives.

"Perfect," he said as he wound the film, listening to the blonde slam out his front door, and popped it out into his hand. He'd have to remember to reload before he went out tomorrow.

He placed the camera back underneath his bed and lay down. Through his open window he could hear the city, and pictured it, going on outside his head. All of the people, living their lives. Each one with a target on their face.

Quarry
First Prize

By Deborah Pearson-Jones

How you make your crossbow. Some three-by-two from a building site. Make a crucifix. Get some thick rubber; nail the rubber along the cross-piece. Use nails each end, either side of the rubber then smash them over the rubber till it squishes down. Now, on the rifle bit, the bit you point, put a clothes peg. That's how you hold the rubber when you pull it back.

The arrows have to be about six inches long. Make an end pointy, and at the other end cut a cross so you can slip the flights in. You can make neat flights with cardboard.

To load up, put the front of the crossbow on the floor, use your foot to hold it, then pull the rubber back, click it into the peg. But don't put the bolt in, just have it ready. When you want to fire, stick it on then.

The crossbows we made could fire bolts more than 200 yards. The record was more than five hundred yards, over the roofs of the houses opposite, over the dingle, over the dump, and slamming into the spongy grass of the golf links beyond.

You'll have to practice. Have to get really good, be a dead-eye dick. You won't get two shots. Practice hitting cans and stuff. You'll need to get used to aiming exactly.

You use your sister. You practice in the front room. You tell Maddie it's the only way. You *have* to get good because otherwise, well just, *otherwise...*

She says, but if you get it wrong I'll be stabbed-in-the-back. She says it really fast, gasping, dramatically, like someone on television, like one of the Swiss soldiers in William Tell, talking to Lamburger Gessler.

You put pillows on her, on her head, her delicate neck and around her back, then tie them on with string. Then you get her to stand in the doorway, face away. You say, "Be still'. You put two baby's play blocks on her head, one on top of the other, but she moves. They fall off.

"Stand still!" you shout. You sound like your father. She flinches.

The second time she stands rock-steady.

You've hung a curtain in the doorway, to catch the bolts when you miss. You aim deliberately high, thinking you will work your way down, practice, get good at shooting, but the first shot goes straight through the curtain into the hall and thuds into the hanging coats.

"Wow!" Indoors, the power of the bow staggers you. You begin to think you have real strength, that you *can* fight back. Maddie has moved and the blocks are on the floor. You tell her, Maddie it's going to work, and you pick up the blocks, put them on her head, stand back, and load up the crossbow, put in a second bolt.

"OK?"

She says OK, but it's long and drawn out, almost a question.

FLACK!

Second shot you hit the plastic block, and splat, bolt and block fly through the air. Maddie has lowered her head, then she picks up the block and bolt. "Cor Blimey!" she says. Then she says, "Do it again!"

That morning, you shoot about a dozen times. You hit the top block three times, the lower one three times. Twice you're too high and shoot the coats in the hall, once you slam into the pillows, and once, you don't know what happened, the bolt comes out all wrong, sideways, and clatters into the "Bless This House' plaque above the mantelpiece.

You and Maddie are kids. You're tough but you're not stupid. You need to be tougher, bigger, and having a weapon helps. That afternoon you, Billie, Colin Glasseye and Joseph Healey – no girls – you go as a gang on the five mile march to the quarry looking for The Dirty Old Man.

All of you have crossbows.

The quarry is red mud. When dry, the banks of red shale are soft as talcum powder and the bravest boys know how to jump off the edge and half fall, half-run through the falling colors.

At the bottom is a deep pool, blacker than black. They have all seen the surface break suddenly, they have told each other they have seen bubbles, but whether there are unknown fish or monsters in the deep, they don't know.

In the buildings, creepy, drippy, metallic, the boys and the girls used to play often, (Maddie too, before she got too sad) throwing bricks, breaking windows, clanging bits of metal, trying to make old motors work, building dens, playing hide and seek. Until.

Until that once, when The Dirty Old Man was in one of the buildings. They'd been smashing stuff up and then they'd gone inside somewhere to share some pop. The Dirty Old Man was crafty. He had hidden somewhere and waited for them, and when they'd sat down, he appeared in the only doorway, the sun behind him, and shouted, "Right, you bloody buggers!"

He was big, in an overcoat. He had a fat face and hadn't shaved for a while. His eyes were yellowy and the eyelids sort of flopped open showing some of the red insides. He had filthy hands and filthy nails that showed through his gloves, the kind that had no fingers.

"Nasty little sods! I'll "ave yer! Come ere!"

You all freeze, but not forever. You are kids from up the Gaer and you don't mess about. Billie pushes you left and you grab the nearest girl as he goes right, followed by Joseph and the others. Colin Glasseye climbs up on some bricks, grabs one and shouts, "Come on then, Dirty Old man! Come up here! I'll smash yer face in!"

You can't remember how the break and stampede works, but it does. A minute later you are outside in the fresh white sunshine, panting, raising little fists towards the old man in the doorway. It's another minute before you're aware that Maddie is still inside.

It's you who realizes first. Something changes. You don't even think to enlist your friends. You run straight towards the old, too-big man in the overcoat, stop maybe half a dozen feet away, grab a piece of wood. "You dirty old fucker! Let my sister out! Dirty old fucker!"

He's so big he fills the doorway. He's leaning slightly and now you see he's drunk, dopey. He has a squat bottle with purple liquid in it. Even from where you stand, shaking, you can smell it. Then behind, in the dark, you see Maddie, more perplexed than scared.

"You dirty old fucker!"

The other boys come up, shouting the same thing, tentatively braver. This is when the old man steps sideways, turns to Maddie, and waves her out, like a gentleman waves to a lady.

Maddie comes forward. To get through the door she has to go within inches of the old man. He waves again, kindly. She shrinks as she passes, and then, just as she is about to reach the light, he grabs her by one wrist, envelopes her, lifts her up to show his power, roaring. Now she is upside down, her knickers showing. He smacks her arse, laughs, then puts her on the floor where she scurries away.

You all run, perhaps fifty yards, before realizing you lost the battle. You should go back, but you're not sure for what. By the time you've walked most of the way home the story is that a horrible old man had captured you all and tried to do something to the girls.

You're going to get him. One day.

And this is the day. You, the boys, all have your crossbows. All the way here you've been talking about getting The Dirty Old Man, and every now and then one of the boys points his crossbow at a tree and goes "Peeeow!!"

When you get to the quarry, you fan out into the buildings, backs to walls like film-soldiers then scurry across open ground, rolling behind rusty iron, low walls. This is drama. It fills you up.

You close in on the place where soft smoke rises, waving to each other, whispering, hissing, moving forward like Audie Murphy, Alan Ladd.

And then you are there, commandos, and across a few feet of redbrick yard is his HQ. You were voted so you get up and walk forward.

"Hey, Mister!" And when there is no reply, "Hey, Mister!" again.

There is no movement, just the flabby, light grey smoke.

"Hey Mister! I want to talk to you. You touched my sister!"

But nothing.

It's five minutes before the boys decide to go in. You'll go together and shoot him, shoot The Dirty Old Man dead, then carry him out and chuck him in the black pool.

Together, crossbows ready, the four of you, brave boys, stride towards the doorway. In your memory, this image is perfect, except it has to be shot from inside the building for you see yourself striding towards the camera, heroic, determined, trained.

And finally, when you are inside, when you have adjusted to the dark, you see The Dirty Old Man, just *there*, half-sitting, half-lying, a sort of a smile on his face. His eyes are open but he's not seeing you.

You close on him. All of you are shouting, what, you cannot remember but you guess it was 'Bugger' and 'Fucker' and 'Dirty Old Man'. You stop perhaps six, eight feet from him and he doesn't move, doesn't blink.

"Get him!" you say and you all fire.

Four bolts thud into him, into the thick coat, dull and hopeless, dropping to the floor. The other three boys turn and run almost as they shoot, but you don't. You re-load, step closer, take careful aim at the face, and fire.

You are exultant. The bolt flashes into skin_like into cheese, into the old man's grey cheek, deep and peculiar. You stare at the man. He stares back. There is no blood, just a minute slick of something watery and brown on his cheek. You cannot get over how far in the bolt has gone. You reload, then go forward again, and from four feet you fire at the forehead.

The arrow breaks skin but bounces off skull bone, but then, as if the old man is playing with you, he slowly lies himself down on the floor, on the good cheek, the arrow flights protruding from the other side of his face.

You are amazed. You crouch down and stare at a dead man. You poke him with the cross of your weapon and nothing happens. He is no different to a dead cat or a dead dog.

You call the others. You find five crossbow bolts, then you try and retrieve the sixth. It is stuck firm in the old man's face. You need one of the others to hold him while you pull. No one wants to and you shout. Billie and Joseph help. Between them, they hold the dirty head down with their feet and you work the bolt free.

You leave. No longer exultant.

Between the four of you, you agree to tell the girls that The Dirty Old Man ran away. You never hear anything about him.

But, then, one night, Maddie is crying again. Father goes out, slamming the door. Maddie is that special sad, and you tell her the truth.

You say, "See, Maddie?" and you tell her every day you are getting bigger, stronger. You can protect her now. It will stop. She sniffles. Soon, you tell her, but you will have to get it right, probably do it when he is drunk, when he's asleep. The first shot has to be a good one. They might not get a second.

Soon, Maddie, I promise.

The Authors

Kendare Blake is an American writer currently living in London, where she is pursuing an MA in Creative Writing from Middlesex University. When she is not writing, she can often be found on wild and/or pointless excursions, such as spraying strangers with silly string, or almost getting hit by cars while helping turtles to cross the road. She writes novels and short stories, and the occasional painfully bad poem.

Born in N. London, **Susan Davis** now lives in S.Shropshire and has been writing for most of her life. In 2002, the first book of her trilogy for teenagers, 'The Henry-Game' (Transworld) was published. Her short fiction has been broadcast and published in magazines and anthologies, including, Metropolitan, Staple, Chapman, Mslexia, and Best New Horror. She sees the short story form as a place to experiment, free from commercial pressures. It remains a dream of hers to publish a collection one day.

Joanne Riccioni is English but now lives in Sydney, Australia. She started writing short stories about four years ago to create some "head space" while bringing up two small children. She has subsequently won competitions in Australia, the UK, Ireland and the US, and cannot seem to leave short stories alone. She may never write a novel.

Swathi Kappagantula was born in Quebec City and raised in Ottawa. A graduate of the University of Pennsylvania and the London School of Economics, she is a diplomat with the Canadian Foreign Service and is currently posted to Washington, DC. She won second prize in the 2006 Ottawa Short Story Contest, and her poetry is forthcoming in the anthology *Yellow as Turmeric, Fragrant as Cloves* (2008). She is at work on a collection of short stories.

Judy Walker has an MA in Creative Writing from Newcastle University. Her first play was performed in Hexham, Northumberlandl in May 2007. She has won and been shortlisted in a number of short story competitions and her work has been published in anthologies and magazines and broadcast on BBC Radio Four and local radio stations. She is a member of the Vane Women writers' and performers' collective and a partner in Blinking Eye Publishing.

Josh McDonald is a writer and singer/songwriter. He has written two novels, a play and more recently a novella and an interrelated collection of short stories which includes "The Aquarium". Josh is part of a writers group that has toured with British Arts Council funding to promote modern storytelling and has written the lyric score to a short animated film by a Finnish director. He runs a monthly "Folk Tales" short fiction and acoustic music night and is part of the "Heads and Tales" spoken fiction collective.

Cally Taylor lives in Brighton and works in London as a Learning Technologist. Her short stories have been published online (SmokeLong Quarterly, WordRiot, Espresso Fiction, Susurrus) and in print (Aesthetica magazine, Woman's Own, My Weekly and several short story anthologies) and "Full to Spilling" was performed by the Liar's League in June. This year Cally was awarded joint first place in the Sedbergh Festival of Books and Drama and her story "SuperEd" will be broadcast on BBC Radio Cumbria in August. Cally has just finished the first draft of her novel (working title "Diary of a Dead Girl"). Her website can be found at www.callytaylor.com

Helen Hunt works part-time for a national charity and part-time in an antiques shop. She finds time to write in between, and has had a true story published by *My Weekly* magazine and a short story accepted for publication by *Cauldron* magazine. Helen has been writing fiction and non-fiction for the last two years and you can read her blog at http://FictionIsStrangerThanFact.blogspot.com.

Lucy Palmer is in her thirties and teaches English to adults in Lyon, France. She has a lifelong passion for language in all its forms (literature in particular) and also for the great outdoors where she does her most productive thinking. 'Epiphany' is her first story to appear in print.

Sally Quilford has been writing since 1995, and has appeared in two Sexy Shorts anthologies from Accent Press, a Bewrite anthology, Womanscapes, and had stories and articles published in several British and US newspapers and magazines as well as being a regular contributor to Amazon Shorts. Though born in Wales, she lives in Derbyshire. Sally has recently released a collection of her short stories called Eves of Destruction, and is working on a novel which she hopes to release later in the year. You can find out more about Sally and her work at http://www.sallyquilford.co.uk.

The Photographer

Reba Saldanha is a documentary photographer from Boston, MA specializing in people and animals in their natural environments. Her travels include India, Ecuador, Australia, Portugal, Spain, France, England, Germany, Ireland, Malaysia and most of the 48 continental states.

She has been a staff photographer for the Daily Item in Massachusetts for 4 years now and looks forward to more adventures through the lens.

In keeping with this year's theme of transformation, all photos were digitally transformed into line art using Adobe Photoshop. See more of her photography on the internet at www.rebaphoto.com.

The Judges

Lucy Alexander is a writer and researcher on *The Times Magazine*. She read English Literature at Oxford, then worked in PR, becoming an account manager at Freud Communications before moving into journalism at *The Times* in 2001. She says of her involvement in the Momaya Short Story Competition: "Casting judgement on the work of other writers is an honour, a challenge and a big responsibility. I hope the Momaya Comp-etition continues both to raise the profile of the short story as a genre and to encourage writers from all over the globe to participate."

Claire Nozières works at Andrew Nurnberg Associates as a literary agent. Previously she was Foreign Rights Manager at Frances Lincoln, an independent publishing house specialized in high quality illustrated books and children's books. Claire sells translations rights to France for a wide-ranging list of contemporary US and UK fiction.

Alison Hennessey has worked in publishing for five years, and is now an Editor at Random House. She also works as a freelance reader for a literary consultancy.

Momaya Press

Monisha Saldanha Koruth earned her MBA at Harvard Business School in 2001 and has been working in publishing and internet commerce ever since. She believes that building a worldwide audience for the short story is vital to the promotion of this art form, and is proud that Momaya Press is increasingly recognised as the premiere forum for short story writers.

Maya Cointreau received a degree in Russian Literature from Smith College in 1996 and has more than a decade of experience in publishing and graphic arts. Among other things, she was managing editor of *DCC Magazine*, a magazine with a circulation of more than 60,000 readers, and has published fiction and non-fiction works including: "Breaking Eight," "The Book of Cookbooks, Volume 2," "Equine Herbs & Healing: An Earth Lodge Herbals Guide to Horse Wellness," and "To The Temples: 14 Guided Meditations for Healing & Wisdom." She is currently working on two new books, "Canine Herbs & Healing" and "Eden is Now."

Acknowledgements

We at Momaya Press would like to thank every author who submitted their stories this year — the fabulous, the unique, the heartfelt -- you each had a special tale to tell. We encourage you to keep on writing, for through writing you are an integral part of the divine cycle of creation, which keeps our planet's pages turning.

We give great thanks to our wonderful judges Lucy, Claire & Allison, and our pro-bono photographer Reba Saldanha, for joining forces with us and helping to create this year's review.

We also would like to thank our families, for their enduring love and support. You mean the world to us.

www.ingramcontent.com/pod-product-compliance
Lightning Source LLC
Chambersburg PA
CBHW030344030726
47499CB00003B/888